THE WILD DONAHUES

THE
WILD
DONAHUES

Elisabeth
Hamilton
Friermood

Doubleday & Company, Inc.

Garden City, New York

CONTENTS

For
The Butler Girls
Sally — Leslie — Mary

AUTHOR'S NOTE

Years ago my father told me about a house he lived in as a
boy, and about the rascally family that had built it long before
his time, in pre-Civil War days. "The old man," my father
said, "cheated the Indians right and left; charged them one
dollar for one needle, saying that the man who made them
was dead."

This last about the needles, I always remembered, as well
as the fact that the family ran a race track in the 1850s.

In 1961 I visited my home town during National Library
Week. Just as I left, two friends, Marj and Bob Butler,
gave me an envelope of articles they had clipped from Indiana
newspapers, saying they thought the material might interest me.

Several months later I read the articles and was delighted to
find that they were about the same house and family of which
my father had spoken. In fact, I remembered that I had visited
the house with my grandmother after it was in ruins.

The articles the Butlers had collected told of the race track,
the dishonest dealings of the family, and the tragic marriage of
a beautiful girl to the despicable oldest son. Here were all the

ingredients for a colorful Victorian melodrama, with hero, heroine, and dastardly villain.

At once my wild Donahues began to take shape and Sycamore Park became a lively scene, peopled with the members of this family, a family Grant County is never likely to forget.

E.H.F.

I

SYCAMORE PARK

Meg Donahue held to the side of the back seat as the carriage wheels bounced out of a rut. Night had come on during the ride from town and she could see nothing of the countryside along the road.

The fatigue of two days' travel by train and stagecoach was forgotten. This was the most exciting thing that had ever happened to her, she thought. Her father and mother dead since she was very young, Meg had spent most of her sixteen years with Grandma Hartman in Cincinnati. Now, Grandma gone too, she was here in northern Indiana to make her home with her only other relatives.

The friendly old man who had met her in Rollins clicked his tongue at the horses. "Not much farther now," he said over his shoulder. "You'll see the lights of Sycamore Park when we get around the next bend."

"Sycamore Park?" Meg questioned.

"Yes ma'm. Your Uncle Barney named the place that when the new house was finished six years ago." Jethro Ogleby held the reins in one hand and turned sideways, the better to talk with his passenger. "You know about your uncle and cousins, do you?"

"No. I've never seen them. I only know that there are six boys and a girl and that Uncle Barney's wife is dead." Meg pulled her Paisley shawl closer against the chill of the April night. "What is Uncle Barney's family like?"

Old Jethro laughed. "Well now, I'd scarcely call 'em six boys and a girl. I reckon Mike, the oldest, must be thirty-two or so and the youngest, Todd, is all of nineteen or twenty. And as for Adelaide, your female cousin, she's well past thirty and looks it too."

Meg felt a little uneasy. She had been picturing a new exciting life for herself in a family of young people. She had lived alone with Grandma ever since she could remember and often envied her friends their numerous brothers and sisters. Now here she was, being set down in the middle of a group of old relatives. They would probably be as particular about manners and propriety as Grandma had been.

"Have you worked for Uncle Barney long?" she asked.

"Yes'm for quite a spell. 'Bout ten years or so. Ever since he layed out the race track and built the stables."

"The race track?"

The old man made a cackling sound. "You never heard of the Donahues' Sycamore Park race track? My, my, you really ain't acquainted with your kinfolks, are you? Why racing men bring their horses here from all over; from Kentucky, Ohio, Virginia. These parts of Indiana ain't been the same since the Donahues took over."

Meg gave a shiver of excitement. Certainly her new life was not going to be dull! "You're right, Mr. Ogleby, I don't know anything about Uncle Barney and his family. But Grandma made me promise I'd write to him if she passed on. So I did. And he was very nice—sent me a hospitable letter offering me a home. So here I am."

Jethro slapped the reins on the horses' backs. "Nice, you say?" The old man hesitated. "*Nice* ain't exactly a word anyone around here would use to describe any of the Donahues, especially not where old Barney's concerned." The driver lowered his voice. "I 'spect I should tell you, miss, that in these parts they call Barney and his sons the wild Donahues."

Meg laughed. "Well, Mr. Ogleby, don't forget that I'm a Donahue and maybe I'm a little wild too."

Jethro chuckled. "Glad to know you got spunk, young lady. You'll need it." He turned and gave his attention to the team. "Well, there she be! That's Sycamore Park, where the Donahues hatch out more devilment than you can shake a stick at."

Meg looked at the brilliantly lighted house on the hill ahead. There must be lamps and candles burning in every room, she thought. Shafts of light spread out in all directions from the many windows as though the sun had risen inside the walls and were trying to burst out.

Meg's blood ran fast in her temples as the carriage rolled through a gate and up before the broad porch spread across the width of the house. Never had she imagined herself living in such a place!

The door opened and three barking dogs leaped out across the porch and began jumping at all sides of the carriage. Their barks started a chorus of answering barks from down on the other side of the house. Meg had never heard such a racket.

A man stood on the porch and peered into the darkness. In the shaft of light from the door he seemed a giant to Meg. His voice roared out above the pandemonium raised by the dogs.

"Did you fetch her, Jethro?" He descended the steps. "Shut up, you dirty brutes," he yelled at the dogs.

Jethro cracked his whip at the big hounds and jumped over the wheel. "Here she be, Barney, Miss Meg Donahue, all the way from Cincinnati."

Meg put a hand into Jethro's extended one, pulled her full

skirts through the opening in the carriage, and stepped down.

The giant stood beside her. "So, you're Brother Daniel's girl. I'm your Uncle Barney. Come on in so's I can take a look at you. Jethro, you fetch her things inside."

Meg followed Uncle Barney up the steps and across the porch into the center hall. The lamps in wall niches were turned high, lighting a wide expanse of red carpet, and numerous pictures of horses on the walls. A black leather saddle, decorated in gold bands, was mounted on the main post at the foot of the staircase.

The hall seemed to Meg to be filled with men, big, dark, ominous, staring men. She glanced at her uncle's ruddy face, as lined as a withered apple. His black hair had turned white at the temples. His full mouth narrowed as he pursed his lips and looked her over.

"Well, I must say you don't look much like a Donahue with all that yellow hair and blue eyes. You must take after your mother's side. These are your cousins." He pointed to each towering man looking down at her. "This is Mike, Jason, Chris, Ben, Ross, and Todd. Boys, this is your cousin Meg, your uncle Daniel's girl."

There was a noise in a doorway and Meg saw a woman as tall and dark as the men and whose eyes had the same disconcerting stare as they took Meg in from the top of her bonnet with its black veil in mourning for Grandma, down to the bottom of her gray challis dress stretched out over her hoops.

"This is your cousin Adelaide," Uncle Barney said.

The woman walked toward Meg slowly, never taking her eyes away. Meg swallowed hard. She was being stupid, she knew, letting these cousins frighten her. But there were so many of them in this great hall, she felt like a scared rabbit. Timidly she extended her gloved hand to Adelaide.

"How do you do, Cousin Adelaide. You are good to give me a home. I hope I shall be able to help you with household tasks. For the past year I have taken care of all the house-keeping for Grandma Hartman."

The older woman took the offered hand. "That won't be necessary," she said, and her deep voice sounded as though it came out of a well. "Giving you a home was Pa's idea, not mine. I had no idea you were so young."

From her tone one would have thought that youth was a sin. Meg quickly withdrew her hand in confusion. One male cousin began picking up her valises and boxes. The others moved to leave the hall without saying a word of greeting.

Adelaide took Meg's arm in a firm grasp and pushed her toward the stairs. "I'll take you up to your room."

At that precise moment there was a rustle of skirts above. Meg looked up and saw a young woman descending. All of the Donahues paused and raised their eyes. The expression on the face of Mike, the tallest and darkest son, changed from one of indifference at Meg's arrival to one of sly satisfaction as he watched the figure above. He went forward and waited at the bottom step.

Meg forgot the others as the young lady moved downward with the stately dignity of a queen. Halfway down, the light from the many lamps revealed her to Meg. Her dress of maroon silk swept down from the tiny waistline of the snug bodice into a skirt which Meg was sure must have ten or twelve yards of material in it. The lace of the collar matched the pale cream-iness of her complexion. Her hair was drawn down from a center part, low over the ears. Three brown curls hung over her left shoulder. Her deep dark eyes looked down into Meg's with compassion and understanding. Meg knew that this was the most beautiful woman she had ever seen. Who was she? She didn't resemble the others. Surely she wasn't another Donahue cousin.

Mike took hold of the young lady's hand possessively as

she reached the bottom step and pulled her toward Meg with a proprietary air.

"Cousin Meg," he announced loudly with an uptoss of his massive head and a white-toothed grin, "*this* is *my wife*, Marietta."

Uncle Barney laughed raucously and said to Meg, "Mike's been married 'most a year now, but still likes to brag about marrying a real lady, a Lenfesty. Of course, heaven knows he went to enough trouble to do it. Folks around here said he never would. But hell and high water can't stop a Donahue when he makes up his mind to have a thing." The older man glanced at his daughter-in-law. "Isn't that right, Marietta?"

Meg watched the young woman's face grow paler as she pulled her hand from Mike's and stepped nearer.

"You must be very tired, Margaret," she said with quiet dignity. "You came such a long way. I lit a fire in your room. Come with me." She turned to the cousin holding some of Meg's things. "Todd, please bring those up." She faced Adelaide. "Adelaide, will you please ask Millie to bring supper to Margaret's room. I'll help her get settled."

Adelaide gave a loud sniff, sent a grim look at her father, and proceeded toward the back of the house like a sergeant marching under disagreeable orders.

Meg followed the queenly Marietta upstairs. There was something wrong in this house, she thought, something she couldn't understand. How glad she was for the presence of such a person as Mike's wife. The Donahues couldn't be as bad as Jethro Ogleby had painted them if this nice young woman had married one of them.

Marietta led the way down the upper hall and opened a door. "This is your room, Margaret," she said. "Put her things there, Todd, at the foot of the bed."

Todd Donahue placed Meg's bags and boxes on the big chest at the foot of the canopied bed. He turned and looked at Meg steadily for a moment. "As Pa said, you don't look like a Donahue at all, Cousin Meg," he said with a half-smile. He turned to his sister-in-law. "Anything else I can do, Marietta?"

"No, thank you, Todd. I'll help her unpack."

Todd walked toward the door, then looked back. "Cousin Meg, I'll show you around in the morning when you're rested. Do you like horses?"

Meg's uneasiness lessened at his friendly tone. "Why, thank you, Todd. I don't know whether I like horses or not, I've never been very close to any. Grandma didn't have a horse and carriage, you know."

"Then you don't ride?"

Meg smiled shyly. "Never been on a horse in my life."

"Well, you'll have to learn and I'll teach you. We can't have a Donahue who doesn't know how to handle a horse, can we, Marietta? Mike and Pa wouldn't stand for that." He glanced toward Marietta, who was opening the doors to a big wooden wardrobe at the right of the fireplace.

She turned and Meg saw a shadow pass across her face. "Yes, Todd's right, Margaret. You must learn to ride well if you are to live in Sycamore Park."

Todd's expression softened as he glanced at his sister-in-law. "Marietta speaks from experience. She is also a Donahue now, whether by choice or not," he said quickly as he disappeared into the hall.

Meg was startled. What did he mean? No woman married a man unless she chose to—or did she?

"Give me your bonnet, Margaret. I'll put it on the shelf."

Meg untied the ribbons beneath her chin and removed the shabby bonnet, folding the long black veil into the crown before handing it over. She looked about the spacious room.

"Are you sure it's all right for me to have this room? I could get along with a much smaller one." Meg rubbed her hand ap-

preciatively over the quilted bedspread and glanced up at the
ruffled canopy. "I'm not used to anything this fine."

Marietta put a hand on Meg's arm and looked into her eyes.
"Of course it's all right, Margaret, for you to have the best we
can offer. I have a feeling that you and I are going to become
very good friends. It will be wonderful to have a young woman
like you in the house."

Meg hesitated, then said, "I'll be seventeen in June. I don't
imagine that you are very much older."

"I'm twenty-one." Marietta's eyes clouded. "But sometimes I
feel nearer forty. I have a sister about your age whom you will
enjoy knowing. Her name is Joyce."

Meg undid the clasps on her carpet bag while Marietta untied
the rope on a box.

"Do you have a trunk coming?" Marietta asked as she removed
a dark dress and hung it in the closet.

"No. This is all I have. After Papa died, Grandma and I
had to be very frugal to make ends meet. There was very
little for new clothes. Most of my dresses are made over from
Grandma's things." Meg put her underwear into a drawer of
the bureau.

"Well, we'll do something about that, Margaret. The next
time I go to town you will go with me and we shall buy material
for some new dresses for you. Mike and his father will want
you to have the best." She touched the folds of maroon silk
at her side. "Anything connected with the Donahues must be
richly arrayed," she added with a sigh.

Meg looked at her questioningly, but no explanation was forth-
coming. "I'm sure I don't expect Uncle Barney to spend money
on clothes for me. I'm not used to fine things." She watched
Marietta unpack her petticoats. "Would you mind calling me
Meg. Grandma only called me Margaret when she scolded me."

"Of course I will. There now, everything is put away. Why
don't you get out of your stays and hoops while I go down and

see what is keeping Millie with your supper?" Marietta smiled at the newcomer. "I'll do everything I can, Meg, to make you happy here. Your coming is a godsend to me. Bless you, Meg Donahue." And to Meg's surprise the young woman put her arm about her and kissed her, then left the room.

Millie turned out to be a thin woman of uncertain age. She put Meg's supper on a low table by the fireplace, stirred the fire, and put on another piece of wood.

Meg sat beside the table and took the napkin off the tray. "This looks good. I *am* hungry. Thank you, Millie." She watched the woman fold back the covers on the bed.

"You're welcome. You just hop into bed when you finish your supper. Mrs. Donahue said you was uncommonly tired. Would you like for me to come back and brush your hair?"

"Oh, no. I'll do that."

"Very well. I hope you rest good. And if you was to hear noises in the night—well, just you pay no mind to 'em. There's all kinds of things goin' on around here of a night, but nothing to concern or bother you. Mrs. Donahue told me to tell you that. You just get your sleep." Millie punched the pillows vigorously, then smoothed the white pillow slips. She paused at the door. "I must say I'm glad that you've come, for Mrs. Donahue's sake. That woman's an angel if ever there was one. Good night."

Meg thoughtfully picked up a fork. What was it Jethro had said? "They call Barney and his sons the wild Donahues" and "These parts of Indiana ain't been the same since the Donahues took over." And now here was Millie's warning about strange noises in the night.

She dismissed her apprehension. With Marietta in the house she shouldn't be afraid. And Cousin Todd seemed like a nice young man. But Cousin Mike! Meg shivered in spite of herself. How could Marietta have married him? But perhaps he wasn't as bad as he seemed. Marietta would not have loved and married him if he were not a good man. Or was there something mysterious behind this marriage between the beautiful Marietta and the offensive Mike?

In the softness of the big bed Meg watched the flickering firelight throw dancing shadows on the walls. Never had she dreamed that such luxury would be hers. Imagine, Meg Donahue occupying a room like this! What kind of a life would she lead in this grand house? Uncle Barney was gruff and rugged, but he must have a good streak. Hadn't he given her a home? She would try to deserve it. Maybe when she got to know the Donahues, she wouldn't be so scared of them.

Thank goodness for Marietta!

II

MRS. STOWE'S BOOK

The room was bright with sunlight when Meg wakened the next morning. She stretched her arms overhead, reveling in the downy softness of the bed. She examined the ruffles of the canopy above and thought of the work someone had done, ironing them to such starched, crispy fullness.

She began murmuring softly a morning ritual she had often followed since she was ten. "I am Meg Donahue. Today is Wednesday, April the fourteenth, eighteen hundred and fifty-eight. I am sixteen years old. Whatever you have in mind for me today, Lord, I am ready!" She tossed back the covers and hopped down from the high bed.

A clock began to strike somewhere. She counted the deep, resounding tones. Eight o'clock! Good gracious! Back in Cincinnati she would have washed the dishes, made the beds, and have started washing or ironing or housecleaning by this time. Oh, what indolence! What luxury!

The room was chilly, so she took her shawl from the closet, put it about her shoulders, and went to the windows to see Sycamore Park by day.

From the high vantage of the hilltop on which the house

stood she could see down into a valley which stretched out to
the east on an even, flat plain. There, laid out in a symmetrical
oval, the Sycamore Park race track circled a grassy plot like a
dusty necklace. Even now, as Meg watched, a horse and rider
galloped into view around a clump of trees that grew within
the circumference of the track. Farther left and on the other
side of the track she could see the many stables, all painted
white. What a lot of barns, she thought, and what a great
many horses Uncle Barney must have. Several of them were
being led out to the track now by stable boys. The horses were
getting their morning exercise, she supposed. Two buggies drove
into view from the main road, followed by three men on horseback.

The scene was so engrossing that Meg forgot her cold feet
and the hunger pains in her stomach. Only when the clock
outside chimed out one stroke did she give a start. That must
be half-past eight! She had been standing at the window watching the activities at the stables and on the track for half an
hour!

Hastily she began to dress. She brushed her blond hair,
twisted it into a wide knot on her neck, and put on a strong
net to hold it in place. She looked in the mirror and wished her
hair curled like Marietta's, so that she might have curls over her
shoulder too. It was so stylish to wear one's hair that way. But
Grandma had said she was lucky to have a few curly strands
above her forehead. Meg sighed. She wished Grandma were
here so she could talk over this extraordinary house, its grounds,
and the overwhelming Donahues.

She opened her door softly and looked up and down the
hall. There was no one in sight. At the top of the stairs she
listened. There was no sound as she descended.

Below she inspected the big entry hall, remembering the scene
there last night. Where were Uncle Barney and his six towering sons this morning? Probably down at the stables. And

Adelaide, where was she? Meg noted several doors opening off the hall and half expected to see her dour-faced cousin enter to view her disapprovingly.

Meg went closer to the walls and inspected the framed engravings hung there, all pictures of horses. She read the printing below each one. These must be famous race horses, she judged. What queer names they had: Diomed, Sir Archy, Sir Henry, Eclipse, Gray Eagle, Boston, Duroc. No doubt her racing cousins knew all about these horses, when and where they had raced and the time they had made on the track. Now that she was living here, maybe she should learn what she could about horses and racing. From what she had seen at the window, it appeared that life at Sycamore Park revolved around the race track. Did Marietta take an interest in this Donahue preoccupation with horses?

She wandered through an open door into a large room furnished with chairs, settee, table, small taborets, and a sofa. A fire blazed in the deep fireplace. The sun, coming through the far window, flashed across the white and black keys of a melodeon in that end of the room. The floor was covered by a green carpet, liberally decorated with white and yellow roses.

Such a sumptuous parlor! Meg thought. How queer to have the shutters open with the sun glaring in to fade the carpet, and a fire in the fireplace too! Back home, Grandma had always kept their tiny parlor shuttered and closed, to be used only for company. It appeared that this one was used every day. Uncle Barney certainly lived in a grand manner.

Back in the hall, she meandered into a smaller room on the other side, not quite so elaborately furnished as the parlor, but here too a fire burned in the fireplace. Meg rubbed her hand over a dark walnut table near a window; not a speck of dust. Either they had a lot of servants at Sycamore Park or Marietta and Adelaide had been up early putting the house in order. Where were the dining room and kitchen? She was getting so hungry she would be chewing on a chair back soon if she didn't get something to eat. She wondered if she should explore further.

Hearing the outside door in the hall open, she stepped out of the room in time to see Marietta enter. Her cousin's wife was dressed in a dark-green broadcloth riding habit and a small green hat was perched on her brown hair. Meg had seen such costumes pictured in *Godey's Lady's Book,* but never a woman actually wearing one.

"Good morning, Meg." Marietta smiled at her. "You look rested. I meant to be back sooner. Have you had breakfast?"

"No, I haven't," Meg confessed. "I was just about to look for the kitchen. I'll get my own breakfast. I don't want to cause anyone trouble."

"Oh, I'm sorry. I supposed Adelaide would see to your wants. Come along." Marietta removed her gloves and hat and placed them on the table. She led the way back through the hall, past the staircase. She held a door open and Meg entered a narrow passageway. The odor of cooking rushed out to fan her hunger to greater intensity. The rattle of pans was all but drowned out by the sound of a voice raised in song.

> "I would not die in summer time,
> And lie within the tomb,
> When blushing fruits are in their prime
> And fields are in their bloom."

Marietta opened the door to the kitchen. Meg's eyes went wide at the size of it. It was even larger than the big parlor she had just inspected. The air in the kitchen was deliciously scented with the aroma of baking bread and roasting meat. A great fireplace dominated one end, while a cookstove reigned at the other. Standing at the enormous table in the center was the fattest woman Meg had ever seen. At the sight of Marietta she stopped her song, and the smile that formed on her lips sent lines in all directions, making hills and valleys in the flesh of her jolly moon face.

"Mrs. Donahue!" she exclaimed. "You look as fresh and lovely as this spring morning itself. You have a good ride? Been over to see your ma?"

Marietta nodded and put an arm about Meg's shoulder. "Meg, this is Tilda Ridenour, the best cook in Indiana. Tilda, this is Mr. Barney's niece, Meg Donahue. She has come from Cincinnati and will be living here from now on."

The large woman wiped her hands on her apron as she looked Meg over. She turned to Millie, who was kneeling at the cookstove oven. "You're right, Millie, she don't favor the Donahues at all." She turned back to the newcomer. "I'm that glad you've come, Miss Meg. Mrs. Donahue needs a young woman to talk to in this house, always so full of men." Tilda put her hands on her broad hips, cocked her head on one side and said, "Land o' Goshen, you haven't had a mouthful of food this day! You must be plumb starved!"

Meg laughed. "I am, I am. And the good smells out here are making me hungrier by the minute."

Tilda turned toward the fireplace, where a small girl was turning three hams on a long spit over the fire. "Lizzie, set places for the ladies in the dining room."

"Yes, Ma." The girl skipped lightly to the cupboard and took out dishes, knives, and forks.

"Set our places out here, Lizzie," Marietta directed.

"Yes, Mrs. Marietta," Lizzie said, complying with alacrity.

"Is Lizzie your daughter?" Meg asked, watching the cook slice a big ham.

Tilda nodded. "Yes, she's my one and only. Her pa went off to California in '49 when she was one year old and we've not seen hide nor hair of him since. She's real handy here in the kitchen. Millie and me depend on her quite a lot."

"Don't cook any ham for me, Tilda," Marietta said. "I ate a small breakfast at seven." She saw Millie buttering the tops of the bread loaves just taken from the oven. "But Millie, I would like to have the crusty end slice of one of those loaves. It smells so good."

Meg did full justice to the ham, eggs, hot bread and butter, and coffee that Tilda put before her. Marietta sipped coffee and crunched the crusty bread. She glanced toward the fireplace, where Lizzie again turned the sizzling hams on the spit, then back at Tilda at the other side of the table.

"Tilda, you're stuffing chickens and geese for roasting and cooking hams too? How many are there to be at dinner?"

"Law, honey, there won't be a mite too much. Mr. Mike told me there'll be five gentlemen from Kentucky and two from over the Illinois line to take one o'clock dinner with us."

Marietta stood up and looked down at Meg. "I think I shall get out of my riding habit. After dinner," she went on, "I'm going to drive you to my home. I was there this morning and told my family about you. Joyce made me promise to bring you."

"How far is it?" Meg asked.

"About four miles." Marietta turned to leave.

Suddenly, before Marietta reached the door to the passage-way, the outside door was flung open and Mike Donahue stepped in like a black cloud dropped on the horizon. His eyes moved across the kitchen and Meg saw his mouth spread in an unpleasant grin as he looked at his wife. He walked swiftly past the table and Meg's nose curled in distaste at the horsy smell of him. His boots, wet with mud and barn filth, made dirty tracks across the clean floor boards.

"Dear wife," he said in a tone of feigned endearment, "help me off with my boots." He sat down near the fireplace and stuck out a booted foot.

Marietta hesitated briefly, then crossed the room and knelt before her husband. Meg watched, fascinated, yet dismayed at the sight as Marietta's white hands grasped the muddy boots and pulled them off. Mike stood up in his sock feet and looked down at his wife, still kneeling.

"Clean them," he ordered.

Marietta rose, stood imposingly erect and looked into his malevolent face. Meg saw a flush rise to her cheeks. "Very well, Mike," she said in a low voice.

Mike walked to the door, then turned, his hand on the knob. "Wish your fancy friends in Rollins could have seen that. They'd never believe it; a Lenfesty taking off a Donahue's boots."

Meg gave an inaudible gasp. Mike actually seemed to enjoy the sight of his wife's hands covered with barnyard grime and the skirt of her riding habit revoltingly soiled. Why had Marietta married such a man? Living on the next farm, she must have known the kind he was. Why indeed?

As he disappeared into the hall, Mike gave a laugh that made Meg wince.

Marietta reached for the boots. Ten-year-old Lizzie stepped from the chimney corner, where she had retreated upon Mike's entrance. "No, no, Mrs. Marietta! Don't touch them. I'll clean them."

"That's a good girl," her mother nodded from the table. "Mrs. Donahue, you just run along and get cleaned up. There was no call for him to do that. No call at all!"

Millie opened the top of the cookstove with a clatter and put in a piece of wood, muttering all the while. Meg thought she said something about a Donahue devil, but she couldn't be sure.

Marietta stood at the door. "Thank you, Lizzie. Tilda, may Lizzie go with us this afternoon? She could see her grandmother while Meg and I visit my family."

"'Course she can. Thank you, Mrs. Donahue. I suppose I do keep her tied too close to this kitchen and forget she is a child.

But, law, in this world a body's got to learn to earn his keep when he's young, else'n he'll go hungry come old age."

Meg finished her breakfast thoughtfully after Marietta had gone.

The grandfather clock in the upstairs hall struck ten as Meg returned to the front of the house. Adelaide came out of the small sitting room.

"Good morning, Cousin Adelaide," Meg said hesitantly, wondering if her cousin would be any better disposed toward her this morning. But even Adelaide didn't seem as forbidding as she had last night.

Adelaide nodded briefly. "Did you have some breakfast?"

"Oh, yes. Tilda fed me very well. I have never seen such a beautiful house. I'm not used to such a fine place. I do hope you will let me help with the work," she added earnestly. "I'd like very much to feel that I earned my salt."

"Very well, I'll tell Millie you are to help her with the dusting." Adelaide went to the wall and straightened a picture. "Todd left word that he would be at the blacksmith shop and if you wanted to come down he would show you around."

"How nice of him to remember. I'll run up and get my shawl." Meg turned to the stairs, then looked back at Adelaide. "But just where is the blacksmith shop? There are so many buildings down there near the race track."

"Come into the parlor and I'll show you from the window." Adelaide led the way and pointed out the location of the blacksmith shop.

Back in the hall, the older woman opened a closet door under the stairway and took out a long black cape. "Wear this, Meg," she said. "I keep it here to wear down at the stables. It will cover your dress and keep off some of the smell which always clings to one's clothes after a trip down there. It seems as though I spend half my time fighting the odor of horses. I don't mind it when I'm at the stables, but I do hate it in the house. Tell

Todd to show you Harriet's colt. Harriet is my mare and I'm as proud of that colt as she is."

Meg looked at Adelaide in surprise. The woman's face had softened as she spoke of the horse. Cousin Adelaide couldn't be as cold and unresponsive as she had seemed last night if she felt like this about a horse. Meg clasped the cape around herself and fastened the collar.

"Thank you Adelaide. I have a lot to learn about horses and racing. If I'm to live at Sycamore Park I guess I'd better start learning."

Adelaide nodded. "Yes, if you want Pa and the boys to approve of you, you will have to learn your ABCs of horsemanship. Todd will help you. You can trust Todd," she added.

Outside, Meg stood for a moment on the broad front porch and gazed down the hill at the track and stables. She breathed deeply. What a glorious morning and what a place! What a place! The grass was pale spring green, several maple trees had budded into the same delicate hue, and the lilac bush at the end of the porch was covered with tiny leaves. Meg lifted her skirts and ran down the steps, across the roadway in front of the porch, and down the grassy slope of the hill as though the spring had worked the same miracle in her as it had in the trees and lilac bush. Adelaide's cape rippled out behind her. She hadn't felt this exuberant since she was a child.

The ground was resilient to her feet and added to her sensation of buoyancy. How good to have room to stretch one's legs. Cincinnati was never like this! Sycamore Park was magnificent and, in spite of her misgivings about Uncle Barney and his sons, she felt fortunate to be here.

Reaching the bottom of the hill, Meg slowed down to a sedate walk. Even before she came to the blacksmith shop, she could hear the hammer on the anvil. Several men stood near the wide-open door. Three horses were tethered at a hitching rail to be shod. Inside she could see the sparks as the smithy shaped a white-hot iron shoe with his hammer.

Todd came out. "Thought you weren't coming," he said as he looked at her approvingly. "You look rested."

"I feel fine. Who wouldn't on a morning like this?" Meg brushed back the curls on her forehead. The run down the hill had set them awry.

"I see you're wearing Addie's stable cape, as she calls it." Todd set his hat on the back of his head. Meg thought this cousin of hers rather handsome, with his black hair and deep-set eyes.

"Yes. She said I should wear it to protect my clothes from, from——" Meg hesitated.

"From the horsy smells?" Todd laughed. "Poor Addie, she fights a losing battle against the stink of the barns. She's fond of horses but hates the smell. Her brothers are a trial to her. Now, let's see, suppose we start with the Donahue string of race horses. Then I'll show you those belonging to our visitors, here for tomorrow's races. I must say the Kentuckians brought up some fine competition this morning."

Meg walked beside him from barn to barn. What an enormous place this was! She had never dreamed that Uncle Barney was so prosperous. Horse racing must be lucrative. And the horses were so beautiful! Todd showed her his sister's mare, Harriet, and her colt.

Meg laughed at the ungainly appearance of the young one. "You won't laugh at him for long," Todd said as they looked over the side of the stall. "He's got good blood. His sire is Sultan. He'll show all of them his heels in a few years or I miss my guess." Todd rubbed the mare's nose affectionately. "Good girl, Harriet," he said, "I'll turn you and your son out to pasture tomorrow and you can teach him to stretch his legs."

"I wonder for whom Adelaide named her horse?" Meg asked curiously.

"I don't know, you'll have to ask her."

"Well, it might be for Harriet Lane, President Buchanan's niece, who is his hostess in the White House. Or it might be for Mrs. Stowe. Have you read Harriet Beecher Stowe's book, *Uncle Tom's Cabin?*" Meg looked up at Todd.

"No, but I've heard of it. I'm not much of a reader, Meg," he apologized. "Mama used to keep me at my books when she was alive, but since Pa took over my raising, horses have been just about my whole life."

"I guess everyone has heard of Mrs. Stowe and her book by now." Meg followed Todd toward the door. "She used to live in Cincinnati, you know. I'm glad Indiana is a free state. I would hate to live where there was slavery. When a person reads *Uncle Tom's Cabin* his blood just boils at the thought of slavery in this country."

Todd raised his eyebrows at her vehement tone. "So? I guess I haven't thought much about it. Some of our racers from Kentucky bring their slaves with them. But I never noticed that they mistreated them."

"Well, you must read Mrs. Stowe's book, Todd Donahue, that's all I can say. And then we'll see how you feel about it!" Meg stated emphatically.

III

RACING DAY

There were seventeen around the big dining-room table at one o'clock, seven strange men and the Donahues. Meg, Marietta, and Adelaide assisted Millie with the serving. Meg was impressed by the soft-spoken politeness of the gentlemen from Kentucky. However, it may have been because their manners and speech were in such contrast to those of her male relatives.

Of course, Todd was the exception. He thanked her politely every time she passed him a dish or filled his coffee cup. The other Donahues ignored those who served them. Uncle Barney's table manners were abominable. Grandma Hartman would have had a fit, Meg thought, if she could see him pour coffee in his saucer to cool and hang his head near his plate as he shoveled in the food.

The table talk was of horses, their care, their racing times, their sires, their dams. Meg listened attentively, trying to assimilate the unfamiliar terminology. She had had no idea there was so much to learn about race horses.

As the men left the table she heard her cousin Jason say to the men from Illinois, "How about a game tonight?"

"Sure, if the stakes aren't too high," one replied.

Jason's eyes narrowed slightly. "You can name them. Maybe your jockeys would like to join the game."

"No. They need their sleep before a race."

What kind of a game did Jason mean? Meg wondered as she helped clear the table. Something that involved gambling, no doubt, because the man had mentioned stakes. Meg was sure that if Grandma had known the sort of things that went on at Sycamore Park she would not have suggested that her granddaughter contact Barney Donahue.

But Grandma was gone and now Meg was a member of this family that Jethro called the wild Donahues. Of course, she didn't approve of all that she saw, but she had to admit that she found them exciting. She must be wary, though, for Grandma had warned her that the devil could take some very interesting and attractive disguises.

In the afternoon Jethro brought a carriage around to the front door. He nodded affably to Meg as he got out of the front seat and handed the reins to Marietta.

"You get settled, Miss Meg?" he asked. Meg nodded. He looked up at Marietta. "This young lady'll make nice company for you, Mrs. Donahue."

"She will indeed," Marietta replied.

"I'm glad she's come, for your sake," the old man added.

At this point Lizzie ran around the house and climbed into the back seat. Marietta skillfully guided the high-stepping horse from the circular drive in front of the house into the long lane that led out of Sycamore Park to the Pike.

Meg wished that she had the courage to ask the many questions that rose to her mind. But there was something in Marietta's reserve that kept her from trying to probe the incongruity of the older girl's presence at Sycamore Park.

They had ridden about three-quarters of a mile on the Pike when Meg saw a big sprawling house.

"Who lives there?" she asked.

"That's still a part of Sycamore Park, where the jockeys and horse owners sleep while they are here," Marietta replied. "It used to be the Donahue residence before they built the big house."

Shortly before reaching the Lenfesty farm they came to the tollgate. The keeper was Tilda's mother, Mrs. Eakins, who was as thin and wiry as Tilda was fat. She bustled out and pulled the rope to raise the gate that blocked the road.

Lizzie jumped down. "Grandma, I came for a visit."

"Glad to see you, child. Good afternoon, Mrs. Marietta. Going over to your folks again?" The old lady took the toll fee from Marietta's outstretched hand.

"Yes. Mrs. Eakins, this is Meg Donahue, a cousin from Cincinnati, who has come to live with us."

Mrs. Eakins gave Meg an appraising glance. "So—you're another Donahue! Seems like we got a swarm of 'em in these parts already. Though I must say you don't have the look of the others."

As they left the tollgate Meg wanted to ask, "Marietta, why did you marry Mike Donahue?"

But Marietta began describing the members of her own family almost the minute the horse started on. She spoke rapidly, her face slightly flushed, as though she feared Meg might ask such a question.

The Lenfesty farm was extremely modest compared to Sycamore Park. Meg liked Marietta's soft-spoken mother and vivacious Joyce, the sister who was about Meg's age. There were four other children ranging down to nine.

Joyce took Meg out to the barn to see a new litter of puppies in an empty stall. While they knelt down to pat the wriggling puppies, a young man led a horse into the next stall. Joyce introduced her older brother, Calvin.

Meg's throat became dry and she felt overwhelmed with shyness as she looked up into his blue-gray eyes and said, "How do you do." He was pleasant and polite, finished taking care of the horse, and left the barn. Meg found her thoughts returning to him again and again as she and Marietta drove back.

It was late afternoon when they arrived at Sycamore Park. Several jockeys were running their horses on the track and groups of men stood alongside, holding watches to time them. Tomorrow was the first racing day of the season.

Later, just before Meg retired, Marietta said to her, "Meg, keep close to the house tomorrow. The track and stables are not places for you to be on the first racing day."

Upstairs Meg lighted the fire in her room, put on her nightgown, and sat near the fireplace. This had been her first day at Sycamore Park, probably the fullest, most exciting day she had ever experienced. And to think that she was to stay here, a part of this turbulent, tempestuous life!

She rocked slowly and watched a blue flame leap up in the middle of the yellow ones. She wondered if Calvin Lenfesty would be at the races tomorrow. If he was, she hoped he would come to the house to see his sister. Even now she got all fluttery thinking about him. If ever she had a beau or a suitor, as Grandma would have said, she hoped he would be just like Calvin. But that was silly; she didn't know him at all, had only met him this afternoon.

Meg rose, got her hairbrush, returned to the fire, and began brushing her hair slowly, thinking of Calvin all the while. She wished she had talked to him longer. She wondered if there were such a thing as "love-at-first-sight." Probably not, but Calvin certainly made her feel as though there might be.

With that thought, she went to bed.

She dreamed of riding a big white horse, jumping it over high fences and walls with the ease of an experienced rider.

She rode into a barn where hundreds of little puppies scampered and played on the floor. She tried to guide the horse around them and into a stall, but for all her care, the horse stepped on one and the tiny dog lay dead and still. She attempted to dismount, but suddenly the horse had grown taller and it seemed miles to the floor of the barn.

Then Calvin appeared and pointed accusingly at the dead puppy.

Meg gave a jump from the horse's back.

She was sobbing as she wakened on the floor where she had fallen from the high bed. She rubbed her arm as she got up.

What an awful dream! That poor little puppy! Grandma always said there was nothing prophetic about dreams, that they were usually just a jumbling of one's thoughts before one went to bed. She hoped so. Calvin hadn't appeared very friendly in the dream.

The room was full of moonlight. She wondered what time it was. As if in answer to her question, the clock in the hall struck three. She took the extra comforter from the foot of the bed, wrapped it about her, and walked to the window.

The view was like an extension of her dream in that it appeared unreal, almost ethereal, lighted by the moon riding high in a sky of blue-gray velvet.

She caught her breath. It was worth having a nightmare in order to see Sycamore Park by moonlight. The white stables loomed distinctly against the shadows and the dusty race track was clearly visible.

Meg opened the window and took a deep breath of the chilly spring air. She knelt on the floor, pulled the comforter closer, and put her elbows on the window sill.

She leaned forward. Was that barn door opening? It was, and a tall man led out a horse.

Meg watched as a strange scene took place. Other horses were led from the stable, mounted, and ridden around and around the track.

She could not bring herself to go back to bed. The shadowy figures near the stables, the running horses, the almost ghostly quality of the moonlight, all made her apprehensive. Were those tall figures her relatives? And if so, why should they be running horses at this time of night? And, if she remembered her morning tour correctly, that particular portion of the stables was where the horses of visiting racers were kept.

Meg observed more horses join the others on the track and circle again and again. This was no race, but just continuous running.

Should she ask Uncle Barney about this in the morning? She remembered what Millie had said last night: "There's all kinds of things goin' on around here of a night. You just pay no mind to them." Perhaps this was part of what Millie had meant. Well, it would do no harm to ask. Uncle Barney didn't have to tell her if he didn't want to.

The clock struck half past. Meg's legs were prickly from kneeling so long. She stood up and closed the window. Back in bed she closed her eyes determinedly. "I *will* go to sleep," she told herself. But the will to sleep often drives drowsiness farther away. When the clock struck four, she hopped out of bed and went to the window again. The ghostly riders were still circling the track.

Why those poor horses, Meg thought, they would be worn out for the races! She caught her breath! Could it be that——? If those tall men down there were the Donahues riding the competitors' horses to tire them, then they were not only wild but dishonest too!

It was almost five before Meg slept again.

By nine o'clock Meg had dusted the downstairs. She had just started toward the front door to shake her dustcloths outside when Millie came down the stairs.

"I have finished dusting, Millie. What's next?" Meg asked.

Millie leaned her broom in a corner and looked around. "You're a fast worker, Miss Meg, and a thorough one. Got through myself in jig time this morning too. Nothing much to the upstairs work on a racing day. The Donahue men always sleep at the stables the night before. They like to be on hand early to get things ready out there."

Meg's eyes narrowed. To get things ready, indeed! "Perhaps I can help Tilda in the kitchen," she suggested.

"I don't know. There'll only be us womenfolks to cook for. All the men will eat down at the track." Millie retied her apron strings. "Law, Miss Meg, I 'spect you never saw the like of the food that'll be on the tables down there today. Mr. Barney's got two men cooks over at the jockey house and they haul vittles to the stables in two big Studebaker wagons. There's an enormous barbecue pit yon side of the track. Meat'll be roastin' there the livelong day and eaten up as fast as it's ready. There'll be roast turkey, venison, calf, pig, and beef, and it will disappear like snow in July when the horse owners, jockeys, and gamblers gather round."

"Gamblers?"

"Sure thing. Betting on the races is what brings 'em all to Sycamore Park race track." Millie picked up her broom.

"Oh, Millie, I wish I could go down and see a race." Meg opened the front door.

"You stay away, Miss Meg. Mr. Barney not only provides free vittles down there, but free whisky too, and by the barrel. It's no place for a lady. You stay close to the house. You hear?"

"Yes, Millie. Marietta told me the same thing."

On the front porch Meg forgot to shake her dustcloths, but

stood entranced at the sight below. The grassy plot in the center of the track was crowded with men, and small groups stood here and there on the opposite side of the track. The stables were alive with activity: horses—bay ones, black ones, chestnut, gray, all varieties—and men—tall ones, short ones, fat and thin.

Millie came out and applied her broom to the steps. "Quite a sight, isn't it?" she remarked.

Meg drew in her breath. "Oh, it is, Millie. I've never seen anything like it. Where do all those men come from?"

"All over this county and the neighboring ones, and some from as far as Indianapolis and Fort Wayne, I reckon. Most women around here know better than to count on their men for anything on racing day at Sycamore Park."

"How long have you worked for Uncle Barney, Millie?"

"Well, now, let me see." Millie stood at the bottom of the steps and rested her hands on the top of the broom handle. "This house wasn't finished yet and the family was still living over in the other place, the one they call the jockey house now. I had been living in Rollins and taking in washing to keep myself, after my man was taken off with the smallpox. I reckon it must have been '46 or '47."

"Then you must have known Aunt Della, Uncle Barney's wife."

"That I did. And a nicer lady never lived. After the years I spent with her I've often thought that there's more to Mr. Barney than meets the eye, more goodness I mean. Unless, of course, it was another case like Mrs. Marietta and Mike."

Meg descended the steps. "What do you mean, like their case?" Maybe Millie was going to shed light on this marriage at last.

Millie looked into Meg's questioning eyes, turned, and gave the step above a vigorous brush with her broom. "Oh, never mind, Miss Meg." She gave a nervous laugh. "Pay no attention to me. Millie Jessup talks too much."

Meg watched the woman run up the steps and disappear through the front door.

All afternoon Meg sat at the window in her room and watched the races. How she wished she could see them close at hand and learn whose horses were winning. Until today she hadn't realized the beauty of a running horse: the way the animal extended its neck, the way the mane waved in rhythm with the hoofbeats, the way the four legs coordinated with the body in graceful movement, the way the tail flowed out like a gala banner. What a thrillingly beautiful sight it was!

There were a great many Indians in the crowd of spectators. Wrapped in bright blankets and wearing hats bristling with feathers, they were conspicuous among the others. Todd had shown her a building called the Trading Post, where Uncle Barney did business with the Indians. He had come to this part of Indiana in the first place because of the Indian trade. From what she had observed of this family, Meg decided that Uncle Barney's presence here as a trader would not be to the Indians' advantage.

As the afternoon wore on and more and more of the free whisky was consumed, the crowd at the track became noisy and boisterous. Meg wondered why the community permitted her wild relatives to run such a place.

It would be easy, she supposed, to cheat a drunken Indian at the Trading Post. Was that why the Donahues provided free whisky? Oh, if Uncle Barney's family had only turned out to be respectable, nice farmers, poor but honest. But to find herself related to a bunch of rascals who lived off the fat of the land by dishonest means—— She wondered again about last night and if they really did tamper with their opponents' horses.

But just what, if anything, could she do about it? Did Marietta know what went on here? Surely she didn't approve. Meg remembered the scene in the kitchen when Marietta had been forced to remove her husband's boots. That Mike seemed the worst of all. Marietta had lived here for a year, and for all of her gentility, had been unable to change things at Sycamore Park. Apparently the Donahues didn't take easily to change.

There wasn't much talk at supper. Meg, Marietta, and Adelaide were alone at one end of the table in the dining room. Meg wished she could have eaten in the kitchen with Tilda, Lizzie, and Millie. She might have learned more from the talkative Millie or even from Lizzie.

Even in the dining room, on the west side of the house, they could hear the noise from the track. Just how long did this go on? Meg wanted to ask, but she refrained.

Adelaide and Marietta spoke of household affairs. Spring house cleaning was to be started soon. Marietta told Meg they would drive into Rollins on Saturday and buy material for new dresses for Meg. They would take the material to Mrs. Guthro, a widow, who lived in a cabin near the river. She was a fine seamstress, and sewed for some of the best-dressed ladies in Rollins.

After supper the three sat in the small sitting room. Marietta closed the door to the hall, partially cutting out the din from the track. Adelaide sat at a desk and wrote in a wide ledger. It must be hard to keep account of the Donahues' dealings, Meg thought. What a household!

Marietta sat beside Meg on the sofa and they looked at a recent issue of *Godey's Lady's Book* as Marietta turned the pages. Meg no longer noticed the noise at the track when Marietta began speaking of the materials and patterns they would use for her new wardrobe. Never had she even imagined such stylish clothes for herself!

At half-past eight, up in her room again, she gazed out at the race track, fascinated at the sight. Lanterns hung from all the trees near the track and stables, illuminating the reeling shadows which moved about the entire area. She could see the fires blazing from the barbecue pits.

Dogs barked and occasionally a gunshot rang out above the rest of the clamor. Once a dog yelped sharply as though in pain. Meg shuddered, hopped into bed, and pulled the pillows about her ears to drown out the sounds.

IV

BLACK LAUGHTER

Next morning Meg opened her window and noticed that the leaves on the lilac bush below had unfolded further since Wednesday. Yesterday she had been so engrossed with the activity at the track that she had forgotten to look at them. The air was delightfully soft, blowing the sweet smell of spring in her face. The wild Donahues notwithstanding, she knew Sycamore Park was one of the most beautiful spots she had ever seen.

Down the hill all was peacefully quiet. As she watched, two wagons moved into view from behind the stables and several men began loading the broad tables and empty whisky barrels into them.

She left the window open while making her bed. It was disappointing that Calvin Lenfesty had not put in an appearance yesterday, she thought. If he had been at the races she had not spotted him in the throng. But perhaps she would not have recognized him from this distance. After all, she had seen him only once. It seemed a little absurd now, those thoughts she had had about him. Still, his sister had married a Donahue and she, Meg, was a Donahue; but that wasn't much comfort, for she was sure there was something wrong about that marriage. The misery she observed in Marietta's eyes from time to time confirmed it. But oh, she did hope Calvin would like her, and if he did, might not the feeling blossom into something more than friendship?

Later, when her morning dusting was finished, Meg went to the kitchen and offered to help. Tilda looked up from the wooden mixing bowl in which she stirred a dark batter, fragrant with cinnamon, nutmeg, and clove.

"It's such a fine day, Miss Meg, why don't you go outdoors? I always say young folks should enjoy the spring; it's so much like them, all fresh and full of get-up-and-go. Lizzie's out back there, helping Jethro put in my garden. To set a tasty table a cook's got to have a good garden. And with my size it's well nigh impossible for me to get down and put in them onion sets. Lizzie said you met Ma day afore yesterday."

"Yes, I did. Has she been the tollgate keeper long?" Meg asked.

"Ever since they fixed up the Pike and set up the tollgate to pay for it," Tilda replied. "Fifteen years or so. And I can tell you there's not much that goes on in these parts as gets by Ma. Lizzie was tellin' me the other day that she thought her grandma had eyes in the back of her head." Tilda laughed.

Meg smiled. "I'm sure my grandma did." She walked to the back door. "You let me know, Tilda, if you want me to help you."

"That I will, Miss Meg. Nice to know there's another pair of willing hands. There'll be plenty to do soon when Miss Adelaide starts the spring cleaning. The whole house will be upside down." Tilda greased the cake pan.

Outside Meg walked down a stone path to the big garden plot on the west side of the house. Here she found Jethro and Lizzie on their knees putting in the onion sets.

"Good morning. May I help?" Meg asked Jethro.

He looked up at her. "Good morning to you, Miss Meg. Oh, there's no need you dirtying your skirts. Lizzie and I can finish here. But it just seems as though Tilda is forever plaguing me with chores like this when I'm needed at the barns. Howsomever, it's Mr. Barney's orders. So, no matter if it's racing day, or if a mare's foalin', or if horse traders arrive, Old Jethro Ogleby's got to dance when Tilda cracks the whip."

Lizzie giggled. "Oh, Jethro, I'd love to see you dance. You'd look funny."

"Hoity-toity there, Lizzie Ridenour. Not more than ten years ago I was swingin' to 'Old Dan Tucker' with the best of them." He winked up at Meg, took an onion set from the basket and thrust it in the dirt. He began singing in a cracked voice:

"Get out of the way of Old Dan Tucker!
He's too late to get his supper.
Supper's over and breakfast's cookin'
Old Dan Tucker's out a-lookin'."

Meg laughed. "I expect he'd cut quite a figure, Lizzie." She reached down and picked up a handful of dirt, crumbled it, and let it fall through her fingers. "Is this good soil, Jethro?"

"Bet your tintype, it is, some of the best farm land in Indiana. Grows everything from onions to oats. Barney Donahue knew what he was doin' when he settled here. 'Course, he didn't buy the farm at first, he just came here with a pack on his back to trade with the Indians. But it wasn't long till he was doin' so well he set up the Tradin' Post down the way and first thing you know he owned this whole passel of land."

Lizzie sat back on her heels and looked up at Meg. "You know what my grandma told me? She said this farm was bought with needles."

Meg brushed the dirt from her hand. "Needles? I don't understand."

"Grandma says that Mr. Barney charged the Indians a dollar apiece for needles when he came here. He told them that the only man who knew how to make needles was dead." Lizzie nodded her head emphatically.

Meg frowned slightly at this added evidence of Donahue dishonesty.

Jethro sent a reproving glance at Lizzie. "Young lady, did anyone ever tell you that you and your grandma talk too much?"

"Lots of times," Lizzie returned complacently.

Further revelations were interrupted by the appearance of a boy running toward them.

"What you doin' up here, Joey? You know Barney doesn't allow you stable boys around his house," Jethro scolded.

"Mr. Barney sent me here a purpose," the boy returned. "'You go up there and tell my niece, Meg, to come down here,' that's just what he said Jethro." The boy glanced at Meg. "I guess you must be the one."

"Yes I am. I wonder what he wants." Meg looked at Joey questioningly.

"I wouldn't know." Joey turned to Jethro. "Those horse traders from Ohio got here this morning. Mr. Barney did some good swopping. You just ought to see two or three horses he got in the trade. Regular beauties, I'd say. And he got rid of Mince Meat and them horse traders never got on to it that he's got an off gait."

Jethro laughed at this and explained to Meg. "We called that horse Mince Meat, 'cause he made mince meat of anyone as rode him."

"But might there not be something wrong with the horses Uncle Barney got in the trade?" Meg asked.

Before Jethro could reply Joey put in, "There's not a horse trader livin' that could get the best of Mr. Barney." The boy nodded with pride. "They know better than to try to palm a sorry nag off on him. If one did, like as not when Mr. Barney found out he'd send Mike or Ben or one of his other sons after the horse trader with a gun. You mind the time, Jethro, when Mike followed that fellow from Kentucky and——"

Jethro got to his feet. "That's enough, Joey. Miss Meg's not interested in horse dealings. You best take her to Mr. Barney as you was told. And you keep your lip buttoned up if you know what's good for you."

On the way to the stables Meg tried to engage Joey in conversation, but Jethro's admonition about keeping his lip buttoned up had had its effect. All she found out was that he was thirteen, an orphan, worked at Sycamore Park stables, and loved horses.

As she stepped around one of the buildings, Meg had a sinking feeling. Uncle Barney, Mike, Ross, Todd, and several strange men were grouped about four horses. Uncle Barney put down the hoof of the black horse he was examining and stood up.

"Sent for you Meg. Got to get you on four legs. Can't have a Donahue walking. This is your horse. Got him for you this morning. What do you think of him?" Uncle Barney took the halter and led the horse to her.

Meg had never been this close to a horse. The animal reared its head and tossed the thick mane on its neck. Meg drew back. Mike laughed unpleasantly, the strange men laughed too, and even the horses neighed as though amused at Meg's uneasiness.

"I told you, Pa, that she isn't a true Donahue. She's scared." Mike slapped the black horse on the rump and the animal sidled nearer to Meg.

Mike's tone of derision fired Meg's temper. Scared, was she? Moving nearer the horse's head, she suddenly grabbed the halter from Uncle Barney's hand and tried to pull its head down so she could touch it. She'd show Mike!

"I'm *not* scared, Mike Donahue," she cried, tugging at the strap. The horse, frightened at this strange creature in wide skirts at his head, reared and shied backward. Meg tried to hang on but the halter slipped through her hands, and thrown off balance, she sat down hard, her skirts billowing about her.

Ross grabbed the halter. Todd helped her up, and Uncle Barney and Mike were joined by the others in loud guffaws. Meg had never been so humiliated.

"Are you hurt?" Todd asked, brushing some of the dirt from her skirt.

Meg's face burned. She looked at the palms of her hands. They were red and smarted from the friction of the halter, and her seat hurt too. "I'm all right," she said.

"Guess you made a mistake, Pa." Ross grinned maliciously. "Cousin Meg is not one of us horsy Donahues. The saddle is not for her."

Another roar of laughter followed that remark. Meg drew herself up to her fullest height and glared at the men. "I'm glad you *gentlemen* find me so amusing," she said sarcastically. "Cousin Ross, if you are able to, please bring that animal closer. I would like to get acquainted with *my* horse."

She stood quite still. If she made no sudden move perhaps the horse would permit her to touch him. The horse might be as scared of her as she was of him. Ross and Todd stood at the head. Slowly she stretched out her hand, touched the animal, and gently stroked the white spot on his nose. The horse quivered and pulled on the halter, but Todd held it firmly.

"Good girl, Meg," Todd encouraged. "I'll teach her to ride, Pa. Mike, you and Ross'll be laughing out of the other sides of your mouths one of these days. Meg will be galloping around Sycamore Park and taking fences like a real Donahue. I'll get a sidesaddle just for you, Meg, the next time I go into Rollins. But you could borrow Marietta's or Adelaide's till then. When would you like to start?"

Meg withdrew her hand. "Why, why, you see—I don't have a riding skirt," she explained haltingly.

"Marietta can lend you one," Mike put in. "So that's no excuse," he added, taking pleasure at her hesitation.

Todd frowned at his brother. "We can't start right away, anyhow, Meg. I want time to get this horse used to the sidesaddle and a skirt first."

Meg smiled up at him gratefully. "I'll be ready whenever you say, Todd," she said firmly. "I may not know much about horses, but I can learn. Thank you, Uncle Barney, for getting this horse for me to ride. I'll try to uphold the Donahue reputation for horsemanship."

"Maybe you will at that," Uncle Barney replied. "The trader I got this horse from didn't give me his name. So, I reckon you can name him. Any ideas? Maybe Midnight or Dark Shadow, him being so black and all."

Meg frowned and glanced at Mike. "No, Uncle Barney. This horse and I have given you and these gentlemen so much to laugh at this morning that I shall call him Black Laughter." Meg turned abruptly and stalked haughtily around the building.

"By Jerusalem, Pa," she heard Ross exclaim, "that girl's got more sand in her craw than we thought. Maybe that yellow hair of hers isn't a sign that she's all wishy-washy like Mike said."

"Time will tell," Mike returned loudly. "She looks like a frightened filly to me, with no more guts than Marietta."

Meg shuddered and ran toward the house.

Right after breakfast next morning, Jethro brought the carriage to the front door and Meg and Marietta drove to Rollins, the county seat, to buy material for Meg's new clothes.

"You aren't afraid of horses at all, are you?" Meg asked, admiring the way Marietta handled the reins.

"No. Horses don't frighten me."

Meg looked at the pretty face framed in brown curls and a blue bonnet and thought, Maybe horses don't, but your husband certainly does. Aloud she said, "Do you think I'll get over being afraid of that horse Uncle Barney got for me and be able to ride him?"

"Of course you will. Todd won't let you get on him until he has gentled him. Todd is a good boy," Marietta added, "very much like his mother."

"Did you know Aunt Della?"

"Yes. You see, I lived on our home place all my life before I was married. Was born there, in fact. I was a very little girl when the Donahue family came to this county." Marietta's mouth closed tightly and she turned her eyes to the freshly plowed field they were passing.

Meg took a handkerchief from the reticule she carried and wiped a piece of dust from her eye. There were so many questions she wanted to ask. If the Lenfestys had lived here so long, they must have known the Donahues were rogues. Then why did they permit their daughter to marry a man like Mike?

Marietta held the reins in one hand and adjusted her shawl with the other. "What colors would you like for your new dresses?"

Meg laughed. "Oh, just any colors as long as they are bright. I've had so many grays, blacks, and browns, made over from Grandma's things, that I've almost forgotten that there are reds, blues, yellows, or purples. What do you think would be a good color for me? You show such good taste in your clothes."

Marietta looked at Meg. "Blue or purple would become you, and you must have something in pink. Then we'll get some bright ginghams for everyday." She gave Meg's drab little bonnet a critical glance. "And most certainly you must have a new bonnet with ribbons and flowers."

"Oh, not so much, Marietta," Meg protested. "Really I don't need all that." The thought of so many new clothes made the back of her neck tingle with excitement.

Marietta patted Meg's arm. "Your uncle gave me explicit orders that I was to get you a proper outfit, as he expressed it.

You must know by now, Meg dear, that the Donahues have everything money can buy."

Meg detected a note of sadness in the last remark. It was plain to see that Donahue money had brought no happiness to Mike's young wife.

Rollins' main street and courthouse square were busy places on Saturday. Marietta drove to Rosenthal's Store on the square and tied the horse at the hitching rail.

Inside the store Mr. Rosenthal himself came forward to wait on them. He was a short, stocky man with a fringe of black curly hair around the edge of his bald head. His dark eyes were warm and friendly as they peered up at Marietta through silver-rimmed spectacles.

"Good morning, Marietta," he said. "Your grandmother was in only yesterday and I was asking about you. What can I sell you today?"

"Good morning, Mr. Rosenthal. We want to look at the dress goods. This is Meg Donahue from Cincinnati, Father Donahue's niece. She is going to live with us."

Isaac Rosenthal adjusted his glasses and stared solemnly at Meg. "So you're kin to the Donahues, are you?" His stare softened into a smile as though Meg's fresh, honest face pleased him so much that he wasn't going to hold it against her that she was a Donahue. "Well, now, welcome to Indiana, Miss Donahue. How nice for Marietta to have a young lady living out there at Sycamore Park."

"Thank you, Mr. Rosenthal," Meg said. "Indiana is a beautiful place. I like it."

For the next hour the store's proprietor took down bolt after bolt of dress material for them to see. Marietta held folds of the various kinds near Meg's face to get the effect of the colors. Meg was almost speechless at the variety of rich material being considered for her. She watched with incredulity as Mr. Rosenthal flipped the bolts over and over, measuring off lengths as they were decided upon. She remonstrated again and again that she did not need so many.

When they drove away, the back seat of the carriage was piled high with packages containing yards and yards of material. There was white lawn sprigged with pink rosebuds for a summer dress, two figured ginghams, one green, one blue, for everyday dresses, a light-green wool challis for spring, a pale-blue silk for a party dress, a medium blue, heavy wool Cheviot for a coat, and purple wool broadcloth for the riding habit.

"Now," Marietta said as she picked up the reins and clicked her tongue at the horse, "we'll go over to Miss Perry's millinery store and get you a bonnet."

"Oh, no! I don't need a new bonnet, and really those two ginghams and the riding habit would have been enough. Will I need a party dress? Do they have big affairs at Sycamore Park at which to wear it?" Somehow Meg couldn't see her big cousins and Uncle Barney attending a party where blue silk would be appropriate.

"No. There are no such parties at Sycamore Park. But my grandmother Lenfesty lives here in Rollins and often has parties. I shall bring you in for some of them, for you must meet people, especially young people. I haven't been to one of Grandma's affairs since——" Marietta broke off suddenly and Meg saw her face sadden and her eyes well with tears. She sat up straighter, pulled a rein, and guided the horse off the square and onto Wayne Street.

Miss Perry's millinery store was next to the Daly Theater. After tying the horse Marietta drew Meg over in front of the theater to read the poster beside the doors. It read,

The Chicago Players Company
Will Present
UNCLE TOM'S CABIN
May 15

"Have you read the book, Meg?" Marietta asked.

"Oh, yes. Hasn't everyone? The play was in Cincinnati two years ago. But even if we had had the money to spare for tickets, I doubt if Grandma would have taken me. She thought the theater wicked and no place for a lady."

"Well, to a certain extent she was right," Marietta agreed. "But there are some very worthwhile things on the stage. I heard Jenny Lind sing right here several years ago. Grandma took me. I'll never forget that. I think we ought to see *Uncle Tom's Cabin* next month. That blessed Mrs. Stowe! Her book has awakened this country to the horror in our midst as nothing else could. Did you have any firsthand experience with slavery there in Cincinnati, Meg?"

"Yes, I did. The city is just across the river from the slave state of Kentucky, you know. And we had a neighbor who often hid runaway slaves in his barn and then took them north in a wagon at night. His wife was so afraid the authorities would catch him at it. She used to sit in our kitchen and cry and carry on to Grandma about it. Did you know that Mrs. Stowe lived in Cincinnati before she wrote her book? And I heard that she gathered much of her material for it from what she saw right there." Meg turned and followed Marietta toward the millinery store.

"I didn't know that. But the scene where Eliza crosses the Ohio river on the ice is so vivid she *must* have seen something similar." Marietta put her hand on the doorknob.

"Is Uncle Barney an antislavery man?" Meg asked.

Marietta shook her head sadly. "I don't believe the Donahues are anything except pro-Donahue, I'm sorry to say, Meg."

"But Uncle Barney can't be all bad; he is providing me with all these things," Meg defended her uncle.

"Yes, dear. But remember, *you* are a Donahue."

V

ON RIVER ROAD

Meg had a feeling of unreality as they drove to the home of Marietta's grandmother. Such a short time ago she was "that poor Donahue girl, left all alone now that her grandma's dead," as the Cincinnati neighbors had said. And here she was, riding in a fine carriage, the back piled high with fine material for clothes for her, and about to make a call at the Lenfestys' big house!

In her youth Mrs. Lenfesty must have resembled Marietta, Meg decided. She had the same sensitive mouth, dark eyes, and queenly grace. She served them tea in her beautifully furnished sitting room and put Meg entirely at her ease.

But one thing Meg noticed, not once did Mrs. Lenfesty speak of Marietta's husband or his family, not even to ask after their health. Was the name of Donahue too painful even to mention? Meg wondered.

Tea was not quite finished when Mrs. Lenfesty said, "Marietta, can you get word to Calvin or your father that we have three boxes of goods for north delivery?" It seemed to Meg that the question was spoken with studied casualness.

Marietta looked straight into her grandmother's eyes, set

down her cup, and got up immediately. "I can and will, Grandma, as soon as I get back. Let's go, Meg," she added abruptly.

When their carriage reached the Pike outside Rollins, Marietta cracked the whip above the horse, and they rolled along at a fast clip toward Sycamore Park. "I want to ride over home before supper," Marietta explained, "and give the folks Grandma's message."

As they drove in past the stables, Marietta called to Joey to saddle her horse. Within fifteen minutes she was dressed in her riding habit and off down the lane again. Meg wished she knew how to ride and could go with her. It didn't seem as though she would ever get to see Calvin again to further their acquaintance.

At breakfast next morning Meg asked Uncle Barney where he attended church.

The elder Donahue laughed, struck the table with his fist, and looked about at his sons. "That's a good one! Eh, boys? I reckon any meeting house in these parts would fall flat if one of us Donahues was to darken its door."

"We got the devil on our side, Cousin Meg. We got no need to go to church," Chris put in with a derisive laugh.

Mike got up, stood behind his wife's chair, and put heavy hands upon her shoulders. "But just in case," he said in an unctuous voice, "we got us a hymn-singing Lenfesty to put in a good word for us to the minister and his church members. Marietta's going to persuade them that horse racing is respectable and that they ought to attend Sycamore Park's next racing day. Isn't that right, Mrs. Donahue?" He put his big head down and spoke in his wife's ear.

Meg watched Marietta's face turn white. "Let me up, Mike," she said. "I must get dressed for church."

Mike stepped back. "You do that. And mind that you wear your new dress and bonnet. I want folks to see that Mike Dona-

hue's wife has only the best. Say," he added, holding her arm
as she started to leave the table, "why were you riding hell-bent-
for-leather across the fields to your pa's last night?"

Marietta glanced briefly at Meg, then looked into Mike's face
and replied matter-of-factly, "I took Mama some thread I bought
for her in town. She needed it to finish some sewing."

All the way to church Meg waited for Marietta to explain
why she had lied to Mike, but no explanation was given. However, Meg forgot the incident during the service as she tried to
still her disappointment at not seeing Calvin in the pew with his
family.

On Monday afternoon they took the materials they had purchased on Saturday to the seamstress who lived in a cabin on
River Road. Mrs. Guthro looked at the various pieces of goods,
took Meg's measurements, and showed them patterns.

It was plain to Meg that Mrs. Guthro regarded Marietta as
a paragon of womanhood. Her admiration bordered on adora-
tion. Mrs. Guthro had known Marietta all of her life; Meg
wondered if she knew why Marietta had married Mike Donahue. Of one thing Meg was certain, she had not married him for
love, and the more she saw of Marietta, the surer she was that
the girl had not married him for the fine clothes he could buy
her. How had such a marriage occurred?

At Marietta's suggestion Meg went to the stables every day
to get acquainted with her horse.

"Talk to him, Meg," Marietta said, "and touch him so he
will get to know you before you get on his back. Ask Tilda for
some little tidbit to feed him, some sugar, an apple, or a cookie.
We don't know what kind of treatment he had before, so it will
be good for him to know that you are his friend."

Proximity to the black animal made Meg uneasy. He was so

big, and when she neared his stall he would lay back his ears and show the whites of his eyes. Todd encouraged her and soon she could hold out a delicacy and scarcely cringe at all as the creature took it from her palm with his soft lips.

She decided that she had been overdramatic in naming the horse Black Laughter and shortened it to a trite Blackie.

Sometimes she stood outside the paddock to watch Todd accustom the horse to the sidesaddle and skirt. She admired the way Todd ignored the laughter of the stable boys and his brothers as, wearing an old skirt of Adelaide's, he mounted the sidesaddle and rode the fractious, bolting Blackie around and around. It looked dangerous to Meg. She was not overly eager to try it and hoped Mrs. Guthro would take a long time to make her riding habit.

The spring cleaning turned the whole house upside down, just as Tilda had predicted. On Adelaide's order the male Donahues slept and ate at the jockey house while the females of the household scrubbed, swept, scoured, and renovated the big brick house from cellar to attic. Meg thought she knew what thorough housecleaning was, having worked under Grandma Hartman's tutelage. But Adelaide Donahue went at the job like one possessed and assigned specific tasks to each of them in tones which forebode ill if they were not carried out to her exact specifications.

All the carpets were taken up and laid on the lawn at the side of the house, where they were beaten until not another cloud of dust could be raised. Lace curtains were washed, starched, and stretched. All chinaware was washed; the silverware was polished. Every picture was removed from the wall and washed. Nothing escaped Adelaide's exacting zeal.

"A speck of dirt has about as much chance in this house as an icicle in the fires of the bad place," Millie remarked to Meg as the two of them, on hands and knees, stretched and tacked down the parlor carpet.

Meg reached for a tack and pounded it into the edge of the carpet. "The house didn't seem dirty enough to me to warrant all this to-do. I must say I'm glad spring cleaning comes but once a year."

Millie sat back on her heels and stated grimly, "I hate to tell you this, Miss Meg, but we'll go through this whole rigamarole again, come fall. Maybe it's a good thing Miss Adelaide never got a man. No husband alive could stand her housecleaning sprees. Good thing Mr. Barney and the boys don't have to live here while she's in one of these pothers."

Meg laughed at Millie's vehemence. "Well, if you've stood it all these years, I guess I can. It's lucky that it didn't start raining until today after we got the carpets beat outside," she added.

"The Donahues get much more luck in all departments than they deserve," Millie commented dryly, crawling a few inches along the carpet. "Now take last racing day. Anybody else set a racing day the middle of April, chances are it would have rained cats and dogs. But not for a race at Sycamore Park track! No sir! The day turns out to be fine and the track as dry as a bone, and the crowd bigger than at last spring's first race. And what happens? The Donahues make money hand over fist!"

Meg looked across at Millie as she pounded a tack in with a vicious whack. "I suppose they bet on their own horses and they won."

"Of course. Nobody ever heard tell of a Donahue horse losing, Miss Meg. They see to that." Millie caught her breath and shook her head. "But I shouldn't be saying these things to you, you being Mr. Barney's niece and all. But somehow you don't seem like one of them, but more like one of Mrs. Marietta's kind."

"Why, thank you, Millie, I take that as a great compliment.

I must admit I don't feel much related to Uncle Barney and the others, all except Todd. He is nice."

"Yes, Todd *is* a nice boy, and given half a chance he'll be good man. But with his pa and those brothers throwing their hooks into him whenever he tries to do something decent——Well, I just wonder how long he'll hold out." Millie pulled the saucer of tacks closer.

"When is the next racing day?" Meg asked.

"It's usually July 4, but this year the fourth comes on Sunday, so the races'll be on Monday the fifth. Not that the Donahues would have anything against holding races on Sunday, but they figure that it might cut down some on their crowd and affect the money they intend to make. The July race generally brings the biggest crowd. Even some of the ladies in town drive out in carriages with their husbands. It's a great day for picnicking in the grove beyond the track." Millie pulled the carpet tight at the corner and banged in a tack.

"Well, good. If other ladies are there, then I can see the races at close range." Meg thought a moment. "But Millie, what if it's like last racing day, noisy and—well, sort of wild? Surely the ladies wouldn't want to be near that sort of thing?"

"Oh, your uncle tries to keep the drunks on the other side of the stables. And he fixes up a special place for the ladies to sit in the shade of the trees yon side of the track. Mr. Barney thinks if the ladies get excited about the races, then they won't object when their husbands come out here at other times. Oh, that uncle of yours is a foxy one." Millie nodded emphatically.

Meg sighed. "Millie, I wish Uncle Barney were, were, well —just a farmer. He's been so good to me, I'd like to be proud of him. But the way things are——"

Millie looked at Meg sympathetically. "There's an old saying that a person can choose his friends but his relatives are wished on him. And how true that is. I ought to know. My own brother was hung for stealing horses about twelve years ago."

"Oh, how awful for you Millie!" Meg gazed out the window. "But speaking of choosing friends, I can't understand how it happened that Marietta accepted Mike as her husband."

Millie's mouth became a thin line as she leaned down and pounded a tack so hard Meg thought it would go on through the floor. "That, my dear Miss Meg, is the mystery of the century. There, that does it." She got to her feet. "Now let's get at the sitting-room carpet. Miss Adelaide will have a fit if we don't get that one down this morning too."

It was still raining in the afternoon when Marietta and Meg drove to Mrs. Guthro's for Meg to have a fitting. Marietta nodded approval as Mrs. Guthro pinned and fitted the snug short jacket of the riding habit above the voluminous folds of the purple skirt.

"You must wear a high white stock about your neck with that, Meg, and I have a beaver hat with a small white plume which will be just the thing. What a picture you'll be, mounted on your black horse! Won't she, Mrs. Guthro?"

The seamstress nodded, her mouth full of pins.

Meg laughed. "A fine picture I'll be when I fall off. I've never been on a horse, Mrs. Guthro."

Mrs. Guthro took the pins from her mouth. "You'll learn easy, I'm sure. Donahues are better with horses than they are with people," she said with an edge to her voice. "You'll make out."

Marietta put a hand on the woman's shoulder. "I hope you and Meg will be friends, Mrs. Guthro. Her coming to our house means a great deal to me. You know Mama won't let Joyce visit me at Sycamore Park."

"Well, I should think not! Not after you——" Mrs. Guthro broke off. "Well, of course Meg and I will be friends if you say so; that is, if she is willing." She held Meg's arm up to measure the sleeve length and looked into her face. "How about it?"

"I'll be proud to have you for a friend," Meg said earnestly.

Mrs. Guthro turned up the cuff and stuck in a pin. "Well, I must say you don't have the look or the sound of a Donahue. Now, do you suppose you could come over tomorrow for another fitting? This jacket has got to fit just proper or it won't hang right."

"I hate to bother Marietta to bring me over again," Meg protested.

"Oh, there's no need for that," Mrs. Guthro said quickly before Marietta could speak. "There's a short cut through the orchard there at Sycamore Park and across the fields and you come out on River Road not far from here. You can walk over in no time at all. You show her where it is, Marietta. I'll need her here often before I get all these things made up for her."

Returning on River Road, Marietta showed Meg where the short cut came out of a field. The rain had stopped but had left the road oozy and soft. The horse's hoofs made sucking, squashy sounds and threw back wads of mud at each step.

"Tuck the lap robe around the other side of your skirt, Meg," Marietta directed, "or it will be mud all over by the time we get home."

Meg complied. "I guess Mrs. Guthro was all prepared to dislike me."

Marietta patted Meg's hand. "Don't worry about it. Agatha Guthro is as good as gold and she knows now that you are too. You two will get along fine."

"It's a good thing I have you to recommend me. The Donahues don't seem to be very popular here. I wouldn't have a ghost of a chance otherwise," Meg returned ruefully.

Although the rain had stopped, it was still gray and cloudy with a threat of more rain. Meg looked at the trees and undergrowth they were passing. "There's nothing as beautiful as spring. I love the damp, fresh smell of the woods. Those trees and bushes are just popping out green leaves all over. Why I can almost hear things growing. I expect violets are up, don't you, Marietta?"

"Probably."

Meg turned toward her companion and noted Marietta's tense expression as she slapped the reins on the horse's back and gave out with a loud, "Giddup, there, Delaney."

"Is there anything wrong?"

"I'm afraid we stayed too long at Mrs. Guthro's and it's going to be dark before we get home. Mike doesn't like it when I'm not home by suppertime." Marietta leaned forward. "Oh, dear, there comes a wagon. This road is narrow and the ditches are deep."

Up ahead Meg could see a wagon approaching. The top was covered with white canvas. "Why, that looks like one of those Conestoga wagons that so many people travel west in," Meg said.

"I wonder if it could be Calvin or Father," Marietta speculated. "They use that kind for——" She pulled the horse to the side of the road and waited.

At the mention of Calvin's name Meg sat straighter and stared at the figure on the seat of the approaching wagon. The closer it got the surer she was that the man *was* Calvin. There was something about the breadth of his shoulders and the tilt of his hat—— She wished she had worn her beautiful new bonnet with the flowers and satin ribbons. But what a silly thought! Wear a bonnet like that on a rainy day!

Marietta raised her hand to her brother. "Hello there, Cal."

The big wagon drew closer, then stopped. "Well, hello Sis," he said to Marietta, and nodded to Meg. "What are you two doing out this way? I didn't expect to meet anyone on this back road." He looked at Marietta and his eyes narrowed slightly.

"I'm taking express up to Ike's place tonight," he explained, "and thought I'd get an early start."

Marietta nodded understandingly. "We've been to Mrs. Guthro's. She's making some new clothes for Meg."

Calvin looked at Meg. "So——? I suppose I *should* know that Barney Donahue would want his niece to be decked out in the best his money can buy."

His tone had a bite in it that made Meg wish she hadn't accepted any of the new dresses bought with Donahue money.

"Now, Cal, don't be critical," Marietta remonstrated gently. "Can you get the wagon past us? I'm over as near the ditch as I can get. I'll just stay here until you get around."

Meg watched as Calvin maneuvered the horse and wagon. Then he stopped the horse, got down, and went to its head. "Got to take this easy," he explained to his sister. "The ground's awfully soft there along the ditch."

The wagon creaked and rattled as it rolled out of the deep ruts in the center, to the side of the road. Meg watched the wet mud fall from the rims of the wheels as they circled forward. Calvin, leading the horse, was just opposite the carriage. Momentarily he looked up and his eyes met Meg's.

At that instant the wagon lurched and stopped. The horse pulled in vain. The right back wheel had dropped into a washout and was over the edge, deep in the mud of the ditch.

"Oh drat it!" Calvin exclaimed. "Now I'm in for it. You and your new clothes!" He looked up accusingly at Meg.

"Why Cal Lenfesty!" his sister said in a hurt voice. "You mustn't blame Meg. After all, the Lenfestys don't own River Road. Just a minute, I'll get out and help." She wound the reins around the whipsocket. "I'll lead Frank while you push at the wheel." Marietta was out of the carriage and beside her brother as she spoke.

"Let me help too." Meg put aside her shawl and jumped

down suddenly, splashing a spray of mud polka dots up over her skirt.

"You girls are going to be a mess," Calvin said as he handed the horse over to his sister. He walked to the back of the wagon and examined the wheel.

Meg held her skirts up a trifle and followed him. Her shoes were thick with mud after a few steps. By the time she reached the back of the wagon Calvin was standing in the ditch, the soft mire ankle-deep on his boots.

"Just what do you think *you* can do?" he asked, looking up at her. "Go get back in the carriage."

Meg gave a loud "Humph!" and stepped nearer. "I can give you a hand on this wheel, Calvin Lenfesty, unless you are too high and mighty to accept help from a Donahue."

He gave her a long look and Meg saw a spark of interest in his eyes in spite of concern over his predicament.

"Well, all right," he conceded. "But you'll get filthy when you take hold of it."

"I'm not afraid of dirt. Come on, tell me what to do." Meg's feet sunk deeper into the ooze.

Under Calvin's direction she grasped a spoke on either side of the hub of the back wheel still in the road, while he stood in the ditch and grasped the other. At a shout from him, Marietta urged the horse forward. Meg and Calvin strained to turn the wheels. They did not budge.

Meg looked across at Calvin. "Let's try again," she said, her face pink with exertion.

Once more they tried. "Relax, Miss Donahue," Calvin said at last. "You're a game one, but it's going to take more muscle than you have to get us out of here." He sloshed through the ditch to the front of the wagon. "Listen, Sis," Meg heard him say. Then he lowered his voice and she heard only a mumble.

Meg looked at her dirty hands, at her muddy sleeves, and

down at her skirts, wet and discolored all the way around where they dragged on the ground.

Calvin returned and said to her kindly, "Thanks for a good try. You get back in the carriage. I'll manage this."

"But if you couldn't manage *with* my help, how can you——?"

"Don't quibble. Get in the carriage," he commanded sternly.

In spite of her dislike at being ordered about, Meg found herself sloshing through the mud and climbing into the Donahue carriage.

Marietta, at the horse's head, nodded at her. "Don't worry Meg, we'll soon be out of this."

In the carriage Meg pulled up her skirts and looked briefly at her shoes, soled in a thick layer of Indiana mud. Glancing back at Calvin, she saw him climb from the ditch and stick his head into the concealed interior of the wagon. Meg leaned forward as she heard the faint murmuring of voices.

In the interim dusk had approached and the sky had darkened further with a threat of more rain. Calvin withdrew from the wagon and returned to the wheel. Meg's lips parted in surprise as a big man climbed from the rear of the wagon.

"Take hold of that side, Sam," he heard Calvin instructing.

"Yes sir," the big man replied and put his powerful body to the task.

Calvin gave orders to the one he called Sam and to his sister. With a quiver and a rattle the wagon lurched forward and the four wheels rolled on solid ground.

Who was this Sam, Meg wondered, and why wasn't he riding on the seat with Calvin? She couldn't see his face clearly as he walked past the carriage and climbed back into the interior, but it seemed to her that his skin was very dark. Could it be that Calvin was helping a runaway slave escape? Her heart beat faster. What if Calvin got caught breaking the law?

Marietta climbed into the carriage and unwound the reins from the whipsocket. Calvin was back on the wagon seat. Meg couldn't see him, but heard him call to the horse. And as the wagon moved away, she thought she heard the faint wail of a baby.

She looked at Marietta questioningly, but Marietta ignored the sound and slapped the reins on the horse's back.

"Get along there, Delaney," she called out.

"Marietta," Meg said hesitantly, "was that man a—a runaway? And didn't I hear a baby?"

Marietta took Meg's arm in a firm grasp. "Meg, you didn't see anything. You didn't hear anything. Not anything at all. Understand?"

Meg almost gasped at the strength of the hand on her arm and the fervor in the voice. Marietta had the same commanding tone Calvin had used when he ordered her to the carriage.

"Why, of course, Marietta. I saw nothing, if you say so."

"And we did not even see Calvin. It was *our* carriage that was stuck in the mud," Marietta went on. "Not a word of this to Mike or the others."

"Count on me," Meg assured her.

When they reached the Pike, Marietta called out in a strained voice, "Now Delaney, let's see you stretch those legs of yours!" She cracked the whip at the side of the carriage.

Delaney did not need to be urged. He was eager to reach Sycamore Park, his oats, and his dry stall.

VI

IN THE PARLOR

They left the carriage at the stables with Jethro and walked up the lane to the house. It was entirely dark now and lights shone from the windows.

"I think we better go in the back door," Marietta said to Meg. "We can take our dirty shoes off in the kitchen and go up the back stairs. Adelaide wouldn't like it if we tracked mud in the front hall. I expect they will be in the dining room at supper."

Tilda and Millie looked up in surprise as the two entered the kitchen.

"Heavenly day, Mrs. Marietta, where on earth have you been? Mike's been on his high horse looking all over for you." Tilda stepped around the table and looked at the girls' bedraggled, muddy skirts. "My goodness! What happened? You two look like you fell in a hog waller."

"We got a wheel stuck in the mud on River Road and had to get out and push," Meg put in quickly. She felt like a character in *Uncle Tom's Cabin*, keeping secret the whereabouts of runaway slaves. She glanced at Marietta for approval.

"Yes," Marietta agreed, "that's what made us late. Is Mike—is he—is he in a bad mood?" she asked hesitantly.

Millie put a pan of hot biscuits on the table and transferred them to a plate. "Oh, no worse than usual. The sheriff's here to supper and I calculate Mike and the rest of them wanted you at the table to put on a good front for 'em."

"The sheriff? Why is he here?" Marietta looked startled.

"Oh, don't worry. He didn't come because of any Donahue misbehavior. Though he wouldn't have to look far to find it, I don't doubt." Millie muttered the last under her breath. "The sheriff's got a man with him, a real high-toned planter from Kentucky. He's up here looking for his runaway property, a man, woman, and baby. I hope the poor souls make it up to the border. But from the look in his eye I'd say it'll be touch and go. He told Mr. Barney that he'd get them before morning. Said he had talked to someone in Rollins as had seen them this afternoon."

Marietta looked at Meg. "Quick, Meg. We must change clothes and get into the dining room at once. Millie, could you come up and help us change?"

"Sure thing. You run along and I'll be up as soon as I take in these hot biscuits. Shall I tell Mike you're back?" Millie stood at the door to the dining room.

"Yes."

Up in her room Meg quickly removed her muddy dress and petticoats, brushed her hair into place, and put on clean garments. Millie came in to button the back of her dress. She held a pair of slippers in her hand.

"Mrs. Marietta wondered if you could wear these since you had to leave your shoes in the kitchen. She said you hadn't got any new shoes when you were in town."

Meg took the slippers. "Oh my, Millie! How small they are! I couldn't wear them. But I have a pair of summer slippers I can put on." She handed the slippers back to Millie. "What tiny feet Marietta has."

"Land yes. Size three and a half," Millie said proudly.

A swish of silk skirts at the door and Marietta entered wearing the maroon dress in which Meg had first seen her.

"Good, you are ready," she said. "Let's go down."

At the top of the stairs she put her hand on Meg's arm. "We must keep them here as long as possible. Understand?" Meg nodded. "Help me all you can with light conversation. I'll concentrate on the man from Kentucky, you on the sheriff. He has a daughter about your age of whom he is very proud. Get him to talk about her."

Meg's heart beat a little faster at the excitement in Marietta's voice.

"I'll do my best," she promised as they hurried downstairs.

Inside the dining room Marietta paused momentarily. Meg saw Mike scowl.

"Well, it's about time you showed up," he said.

Meg watched Marietta in amazement as she smiled broadly at Mike and said, "So sorry, Mike. We got stuck in the mud. How-do-you-do, Sheriff Ramsey. Mike, do introduce me to this gentleman." She swept around the table with a grand rustle of skirts to where the plantation owner had already risen from his chair.

"This is Mr. Cornell," Mike said, and then added with a wicked gleam in his eye, "and you'll never guess who lives on the plantation next to his. Nobody else but John Parrish! Now what do you think of that, dear wife?"

Marietta seemed to wilt right before Meg's eyes. She grasped the back of the empty chair next to Mr. Cornell as though for support and all the color in her face disappeared. Meg was afraid she was going to faint.

Recovering with great effort, she straightened her shoulders and looked directly at the visitor. "Indeed!" she said in a forced voice. "And I do hope all the Parrish family are in good health."

"Quite well, I believe," Mr. Cornell said, as he pulled out the chair next to his and seated Marietta.

Meg took her place beside the sheriff. Todd, seated on the other side, introduced "our cousin from Cincinnati" to both men. Meg noticed that the others were already eating their apple pie. She looked at Marietta and wondered if Mr. Cornell and the sheriff would leave as soon as they finished. Marietta was speaking engagingly to the other guest.

"Mr. Ramsey," Meg said as she buttered a biscuit, "Marietta tells me you have a daughter about my age."

"Yes, I do, Miss Donahue. Got five younger than she is too. Susan's going to be married next week," the sheriff returned affably.

Meg began asking questions and soon the man had stopped eating and was telling her about his family. It was surprising, Meg thought, what a few well-placed questions could do. She had never made such an effort at conversation with a stranger before. But then never before had there been so much at stake. Perhaps the freedom of three human beings depended on the ability of Marietta and herself to keep these two from starting out on the hunt. And besides the safety of the slaves, there was Calvin. What might the sheriff do to him if he were caught aiding runaways? It was against the law to keep a man from retrieving his property.

She heard Marietta ask Millie to bring more pie for Mr. Cornell.

Meg observed that Uncle Barney and her cousins were getting restless, sitting at the table so long. Adelaide looked at her and frowned, trying, no doubt, Meg thought, to convey the message that she should quit dawdling over her food. Usually Uncle Barney and his sons left the table as soon as they finished, regardless of whether the others were or not. But tonight the presence of the sheriff seemed to keep them glued to their chairs. They all took more pie.

At last Mr. Cornell addressed himself to Uncle Barney. "Mr. Donahue, this has been a most delightful dinner. But now I must really get along about my business."

Uncle Barney pushed back his chair; his sons shuffled their feet under the table.

Marietta put her hand on the Kentuckian's sleeve. "Oh, Mr. Cornell, you mustn't leave without a little after-dinner music. So good for the digestion, you know," she added with a coquettish toss of her head that set the curls into becoming movement.

Mike looked at his wife with narrowed eyes. Was he suspicious at Marietta's unusual behavior and talkativeness? Meg wondered.

But suspicious or not, he rose and walked around the table and put his hands on Marietta's shoulders with gloating possessiveness as he said, "You must hear my wife sing, Mr. Cornell. She plays too and we have the best melodeon money can buy in our parlor. Come along."

Other evenings the Donahue sons disappeared after supper, to the stables or the jockey house. But tonight Meg saw Uncle Barney give them a sign, and they all trooped into the parlor, with Adelaide giving their boots a disapproving eye.

The sheriff sat beside Meg on the settee and said, "I thought Mr. Cornell was so blamed anxious to be after his runaways. Well, it's his funeral. It sounds like it's raining again, anyway. Like as not the roads'll be bad."

"Oh, they are," Meg assured him. "We got stuck in the mud this afternoon. That's what made us late to supper."

Mike put a lamp on the organ as Marietta sat before it. She turned some pages of music and smiled at Mr. Cornell, seated nearby. Meg didn't wonder that he seemed to have forgotten all about his hurry. Surely no man could withstand the beauty and charm of the young woman as she appeared at this moment. This was a Marietta that Meg had not seen before.

"Mr. Cornell, this one is just for you," Marietta said as she pulled out the stops of the melodeon and began to pump the pedals.

Mr. Cornell sat forward as Marietta began the words of one of the most popular songs of the day, a song by Stephen Foster: "The sun shines bright in the old Kentucky home."

Meg knew she had never heard it sung so sweetly. Mr. Cornell must have thought so too, for he rose when it was finished and stood beside the organ.

"Mrs. Donahue, thank you. I've never heard that sung better. You actually brought tears to my eyes. I wonder if you'll do one more for me before I go. It is one that John Parrish, my neighbor's son, sings so well. I think it must be his favorite song, he sings it so often. 'Jeanie with the Light Brown Hair.'"

Marietta looked up at the man. From where Meg sat she could not see her face, but she watched Marietta's hands as they dropped from the keyboard and clenched into tight fists in her lap.

Mike got up and walked to the organ. "Let me find the music for you," he said as he shuffled through the song sheets on top. "That just happens to be Marietta's favorite song too. She'll be glad to sing it for you." He opened the music and set it before his wife, then returned to his chair beside Ben. The sly smile on his face made Meg wish she didn't have to claim him as a cousin.

Marietta looked at the music briefly, then lowered her head and began to play. Her voice trembled at first, then came through with tender softness. It was as though Marietta were far away and had forgotten that she was singing it for the Donahues, the Kentuckian, and the sheriff.

> "I dream of Jeanie with the light brown hair,
> Borne like a vapor on the summer air;
> I see her tripping where the bright streams play,
> Happy as daisies that dance on her way."

As Marietta began the last verse, Meg felt tears sting her own eyes. What was the sadness that haunted her cousin's wife? she wondered. Why did she sing this song as though a river of tears was dammed up behind the words?

"Now the nodding wild flowers may wither on the shore,
  While her gentle fingers will cull them no more;
  I sigh for Jeanie with the light brown hair,
  Floating like a vapor on the soft summer air."

Mr. Cornell rose, took a handkerchief from his pocket, and blew his nose. "I declare, Mrs. Donahue, you certainly sing with great feeling. I wish I could stay to hear more. But Sheriff Ramsey and I must be on our way."

Uncle Barney and the others got up quickly as though eager to see the last of their guests. Marietta stood beside Mr. Cornell, the mood of the music brushed aside, as she said, "Oh, Mr. Cornell, it is such wretched weather, why don't you and the sheriff spend the night with us and get an early start in the morning. The roads are very bad. I'm sure your runaways cannot get far tonight anyway."

Mike looked at his wife with surprised displeasure. Meg judged that the last thing he wanted was an overnight visit by the sheriff.

The plantation owner looked down into Marietta's face. "Well thank you, ma'm, but we shouldn't lose any more time. If Sam and Delia were just on their own, I would have caught them before this. But up through Indiana there's an organization to help runaways." He glanced at the sheriff. "Sometimes I wonder if even the law tries very hard to help us get back our property." His jaw hardened and the expression on his face changed from one filled with polite social amenities to one of determined purpose.

Marietta gave Meg a pleading look. Meg wished she could

think of something to say to keep these men here, but as often happens in such an emergency, she was tongue-tied. Thinking of Calvin and his charges, she sent out a brief prayer for help.

As if in answer, there was a blinding flash of lightning and a deafening roll of thunder, and rain beat loudly against the windows.

Meg turned to the sheriff. "Can't you convince Mr. Cornell that you shouldn't start out now?" she asked.

Sheriff Ramsey nodded and walked across the room. "Mr. Cornell, your horse could do with a night's rest. All things considered, I think we'd be ahead in the long run to wait till morning."

Mr. Cornell hesitated, then walked to a window, pulled back the curtains, and peered out. "You may be right at that. Mud holes must be knee deep on the back roads that they'd be likely to take." He turned to Uncle Barney. "Mr. Donahue, if you can put us up for the night, we'll be grateful."

"Sure, Mr. Cornell," Uncle Barney said without much enthusiasm. "Well, the boys and me's got to get out to the stables to take care of things. The womenfolks'll see to you."

All the male Donahues left the room except Mike. He stood beside the organ and demanded that Marietta sing again for the guests. It seemed to Meg that he wanted to emphasize to them that this beautiful woman belonged to him and had to obey him. Meg had never disliked anyone so much as she did Mike Donahue.

Marietta, seated again at the organ, turned to Meg. "Meg, perhaps you would speak to Millie about rooms for our guests?"

Before Meg could reply, Adelaide jumped to her feet. "Never mind, Meg. I've been taking care of things in this household for a good many years and intend to continue," she said with a frown at Marietta as she left the room.

"Sing, wife, sing!" Mike commanded.

Later, in her room, with the spring rain still pounding against the window, Meg went over the whole stormy day. She hoped Calvin had reached the Ike's place he had spoken of and that he and his charges were safe and dry. Would Calvin ever look at her with anything but disapproval? She couldn't help it if her name was Donahue. At least she didn't act like her uncle and cousins. But come to think of it, hadn't she told a big lie this very evening? Hadn't she done it as easily as if she had been lying all her life? She remembered her words to Millie and Tilda: "We got a wheel stuck in the mud and had to get out and push." But that really wasn't a lie, was it? She hadn't said whose wheel.

Meg brushed her hair and sighed. She mustn't fall into the trap of justifying the way in which she had bent the truth for a purpose. She lifted the lamp from the dresser, put it on the stand by her chair, and sat down. She took the little Bible Grandma Hartman had given her.

"When you're troubled, child," Grandma had said, "go to the good book. It'll help you every time.

As she often had done before, she opened the Bible at random and read the first verse her eyes chanced upon. However, it was not exactly chance this time, for the verse had been underscored by Grandma. It was Matthew 25:40: "Inasmuch as ye have done it unto one of the least of these my brethren, ye have done it unto me."

Yes, she had done it for those poor people in Calvin's wagon. It was hard to think of the pleasant Mr. Cornell as their owner. Did he mistreat his slaves as did some of the plantation owners Mrs. Stowe described? It didn't seem possible that he could. And yet those Calvin was helping had run away from him. Perhaps Mr. Cornell had planned to sell one of them and separate the family. If only something could be done about the whole thing, something more than just helping a few runaways escape to Canada.

A schoolteacher in Cincinnati had once said to her history class, "God provides great leaders to serve His ends at propitious moments. Washington, Jefferson, and Madison were born at exactly the right time." Meg wondered if somewhere the man had been born who could do something about this awful selling and buying of human beings.

She closed her Bible and thought of Grandma. What would *she* have said of this new life her granddaughter was leading among her godless relatives? Probably that if her religion wasn't strong enough to hold up in the midst of sin, then it didn't amount to much. Marietta must have had to call on her faith many times to get her through bad times with Mike. Why, oh why——?

Meg got up. There was no use asking that question again. There was no answer. She blew out the lamp and went to the window. Through the rain she could see lantern light in the stable windows. If it stopped raining tomorrow, she would go down to visit Blackie. She didn't want him to forget her. Todd had said that as soon as the puddles dried up in the paddock, she should have a riding lesson. She might take some spills at first, he said, and he didn't want her falling in the mud.

Meg shivered and hoped the paddock would be a long time drying.

VII

THE HANDSOME STRANGER

The sheriff and Mr. Cornell were gone by the time Meg got downstairs the next morning. In the kitchen she found Tilda and Millie doing the Saturday baking. The sun streamed through the window, and the back door stood open. After greeting the women Meg stood in the doorway and looked out.

"What a day! The first of May and everything so washed and green!" She turned around. "Millie, what do you want me to do today?"

Millie looked up from the pie dough she was rolling. "Well, Mrs. Marietta asked me to remind you that you were to go to Mrs. Guthro's for a fitting."

"Where is Marietta?"

"She and Mike left early for town."

Meg raised her eyebrows. "So? I wonder——"

"It's no telling what for," Millie said in answer to Meg's unvoiced question. "But whatever the reason, it'll brood no good for that poor child. The way he browbeats and bullys her is a crying shame. But mark my word, someday Mike Donahue is going to get his comeuppance." Millie banged down her rolling pin hard, as though the dough board was Mike's head.

"Adelaide still upstairs?" Meg asked.

"No. She rode horseback to the jockey house. Said she was going to get them started on spring cleaning over there," Tilda answered with a chuckle. "The men will be as glad to see her as they would a man-eating tiger. 'Course, they could shoot a tiger, but there's not a plague-take-it thing they can do about Miss Addie. Sit down here, Miss Meg, and eat your breakfast."

"Is Lizzie outdoors, Tilda?" Meg asked as she sat at the table.

"Spent the night at her grandma's."

Meg ate the fried mush and syrup Tilda put before her. "About how long will it take me to walk the back way to Mrs. Guthro's?" she asked.

"Oh, I'd say 'bout nigh an hour," Millie replied. "It's a nice walk, through the orchard back there and alongside of the cornfields."

"I suppose my shoes are dry," Meg said, glancing toward the fireplace, where her shoes stood cleaned of yesterday's mud. "My, they look nice. Did you clean them, Tilda?"

"Yes, I did. I calculate they're dry." Tilda poured Meg's coffee.

"It's going to be wet walking," Millie said. "I got a pair of boots you're welcome to if you'd like to wear them. They're behind the door in the pantry. I usually put them on to do the outside chores."

Meg finished her breakfast and put on Millie's knee-high boots. "They fit fine, Millie, and I will wear them, thank you." She put her slippers beside the shoes. "I believe I'll start out right now. It seems so warm I don't think I'll need a shawl or bonnet. Will you show me where I go to find the path?"

Millie stood at the door and pointed. "Right out there beyond the smokehouse and chicken coop, then on around the cow barn and you'll come to the orchards. Along to the right is the path. You can't miss it. There's only one fence and that's yon side the cornfields where they reach River Road. But it's a rail fence and nothing at all to get over. Know your way when you get to River Road?"

"I think so. Marietta showed me where the path comes out, yesterday. I'll try to get back in time for dinner, but don't worry if I'm not here."

"Land sakes! I 'most forget. Todd said to tell you that the paddock should be dry by afternoon and you can have a try at that new sidesaddle he bought you." Millie nodded and smiled. "He'll have you riding in no time."

"But my riding skirt isn't ready yet," Meg protested.

"Oh, you wouldn't want to wear that pretty new outfit anyway while you learn," Millie answered. "Any old skirt or dress'll do to fall off in."

"Oh, Millie! You make it sound awful!"

"Now don't worry, Miss Meg. I never saw a Donahue yet that didn't take to the saddle. Like as not, you won't fall even once. I reckon Todd's got that black horse of yours gentle as a kitten."

Meg made her way around the smokehouse, wondering if she would be able to stick on Blackie's back that afternoon.

The hens clucked contentedly in the sun as she passed the chicken yard; several heralded to the world that they had just laid eggs. By the time she reached the orchard she realized Millie's wisdom in suggesting the boots. She held her skirts high out of the wet grass.

The green fruit trees sparkled here and there with the remaining drops of last night's rain. Tight buds gave a hint of blossoms that would soon open, given the encouragement of a few days of sunlight. There was a moist earthy smell from beneath the trees. The birds, flitting through the trees, did their best to make the season as lovely to hear as to see.

After about a twenty-minute walk, Meg could see the sycamores along the creek, and the jockey house beyond. She

supposed Adlaide was making the dirt fly over there. It was good
to have the spring-cleaning flurry over at the big house. What
would take Adelaide's energy when she finished at the jockey
house?

Past the orchards, the cornfields stretched out as far as she
could see. Newly plowed and planted, the dark wet earth was
waiting for the green shoots to pop up and change it into a
forest of waving green cornstalks.

What a lot of work there was to be done at Sycamore Park,
Meg thought. There were the horses, the race track, the orchards, the cows, the pigs and chickens to be cared for, and fields
of corn, wheat, and oats to be plowed, planted, and harvested.
It was a good thing Uncle Barney had six sons to work on this
farm of his, the farm that Lizzie said had been bought with
needles!

Back home in Cincinnati, Meg had gone to church with
Grandma and felt respectable. Of course, she knew she was
often guilty of such sins as false pride, envy, and anger. But
dishonesty, gambling, and cheating were of another world than
hers. It was not pleasant to suspect her relatives of such things,
especially Uncle Barney, who was giving her a home and fine
new clothes. In accepting all this perhaps she was as guilty as
they.

Looking at this beautiful land it was disheartening to know
that her uncle had swindled the Indians to get it. No wonder
Mrs. Guthro had been cool to her yesterday, and Mrs. Lenfesty
wouldn't let Joyce visit her sister, and Calvin was standoffish to
a girl named Donahue.

She wondered how long it would take to learn to ride well
enough to go off by herself. When she could, she would ride to
the Lenfestys often, so that Mrs. Lenfesty would find out that
she was the kind of a girl who would be a proper friend for
Joyce. And then maybe Calvin——

She came to the rail fence, climbed over, and walked along

River Road to Mrs. Guthro's cabin. The front door was open and she could hear the whir of the sewing machine. Meg had to rap hard to be heard. Mrs. Guthro put her hand on the wheel and looked up.

"Good morning, Mrs. Guthro," Meg greeted her pleasantly. "Hope I'm not too early." She stepped inside.

"Good morning. No, not at all. Fact is, I got the jacket basted and ready to try on about twenty minutes ago. I was just running up the seams in the skirt." Mrs. Guthro got up.

"I see you have one of the new sewing machines," Meg said.

"Yes. It's a Singer. The old Howe I used to have I had to turn by hand, but this, as you can see, I run with my feet and have both hands free to guide the material under the needle. Mr. Singer's foot pedal is a boon to womankind." Mrs. Guthro picked up the jacket from the table. "You walked over, I suppose."

"Yes, and enjoyed every minute of it. Spring is so beautiful. Marietta went to town with Mike," Meg added, putting her arms into the jacket the seamstress held for her.

Mrs. Guthro let out a "Humph!" at the mention of Mike's name. "Wonder how he'll embarrass her today," she said, getting a pincushion from the sewing machine.

"Mrs. Guthro, I've been living at Sycamore Park for almost three weeks and I can't figure out for the life of me why a girl like Marietta would marry my cousin Mike. Why, she's so pretty and sweet, I expect she could have had her pick of all the young men in the county. And from what I've seen of Mike, he's the last person a girl would want to marry if she had a choice."

Mrs. Guthro stood before Meg and pinned the front of the jacket together. She ran her hand over the shoulder and eyed the fit of one sleeve critically. "That one'll have to come out and be cut down a mite," she said. She unpinned the opening. "Take it off."

Meg complied and sat down, watching the seamstress rip out the sleeve and apply the scissors. She decided that Mrs. Guthro was going to ignore her remarks about Marietta and Mike.

Mrs. Guthro sat down, threaded a needle with white thread and began basting the sleeve to the armhole. "Let's see, today's the first day of May," she began, and though she looked at the purple broadcloth jacket in her lap, it seemed that she was seeing things long past. "It must have been three years ago about this time that Marietta Lenfesty began to be the happiest and most in love girl in Indiana."

"In love with Mike?" Meg asked incredulously.

"Land no. She wouldn't give him the time of day then. She was scarcely eighteen and no doubt looked on him as an old man, him being well nigh thirty. I recollect one afternoon that spring she came here to try on a dress I was making for her. She looked so rosy and beautiful, even more so than usual, and I asked her what she'd been up to, joking-like, you know. She told me she had just met a handsome stranger who was lost. He was looking for Sycamore Park, she said. So she had told him the way. I asked her what was so unusual about that. And she said that besides being handsome, he was the most polite, courteous gentleman she had ever met, that he had asked her where she lived and if he might call on her, and said he'd like to meet her folks. He was up here all the way from Kentucky, she said, to enter his horse in the spring race at Sycamore Park." Mrs Guthro knotted her last stitch, leaned over, and bit off the thread.

Meg had been listening intently. At this pause she interposed. "Mrs. Guthro, was that handsome stranger's name John Parrish?"

Mrs. Guthro's head came up quickly. "Why, how did you know? Marietta tell you?"

Meg recounted last night's happenings in the Donahue parlor.

"Well, what do you know!" Mrs. Guthro exclaimed. "My, my, it must have been painful for the poor child. Oh, I tell you, John Parrish was a gentleman from the word *go*. He called on her family, nice and proper, and all the Lenfestys were pleased as all get-out that Marietta had such a fine man seeking her hand. He'd come up for all the races and then quite often in between too. Once she brought him here to meet me and I decided right then that the day Marietta met the handsome stranger from Kentucky was the luckiest day of her life."

"But Mike," Meg put in. "How——? What happened?"

"I guess the first that folks around here knew that Mike Donahue had taken a shine to Marietta was one night in Rollins. Marietta's grandma was giving one of her fancy parties and Marietta and John were there. Tessie Hully, one of my customers, was there too, and she came over here next day for a fitting and told me about it. She said what a handsome couple they made, Marietta in a pink silk dress I had made her and him as handsome as a prince in fawn-colored trousers held down with a strap under his instep, a long-tailed, black coat, and a black satin vest. The folks at the party insisted that they sing. Tessie said it was the loveliest thing the way those two sang together, their voices just seemed to complement one another."

Mrs. Guthro dropped Meg's jacket in her lap and seemed to forget it as she became lost in the tale she was telling. "Well, sir, just before they finished, there was the awfullest carrying on all around the house, shooting and yelling like as if all the Indians on the reservation were there bent on busting up the party. But it wasn't Indians at all, just the Donahue boys raisin' old Nick to a fare-you-well. Old man Lenfesty, Marietta's grandpa, sent for the sheriff and he run 'em off, all but Mike. He hung around and followed John and Marietta home, singing and shouting, sometimes shooting his gun off in the air. He was drunk, of course, but he knew what he was doing all right, just spoiling the evening for that fine couple."

"But Mrs. Guthro, how would such behavior show that Mike had taken a shine to Marietta, as you put it?" Meg asked.

"Oh, that's the Donahues' way. Whenever they want something, they just wave the devil's nightshirt and go a whooping and a hollering after it. From that time on he never let up pestering that girl. Her grandma gave a big shindig of a party to announce her engagement to John, and Mike was outside all the time looking in the windows and making a disturbance." Mrs. Guthro got up and put Meg's jacket on the table, then sat down in front of the sewing machine.

"Did they call in the law to put him in jail?" Meg asked.

"Oh, Sheriff Ramsey can never do much about the Donahues. Around here the Donahues *are* the law. I don't know how they manage it. But it was a dark day when they came to this county." Mrs. Guthro looked into Meg's eyes. "Land o' Goshen! I'm talking to you just like as if your name wasn't Donahue!"

Meg smiled sadly. "When you tell me about them, I wish it weren't. You say Marietta was engaged to John Parrish? What happened?"

"Well, last spring I made her the loveliest wedding dress you'd ever want to lay your eyes on. And she was as happy as a lark. The wedding was to be on May 5. I recollect that on Friday morning, May 1, she came over for the last fitting. She was so excited, for John was coming the next day. She looked a dream in that wedding dress. There was just a little more to do to it, so I laid it out on the bed when she took it off and she said she'd send her brother Calvin over for it the next day. As she went out to get in her buggy, I could hear her humming 'Jeanie with the Light Brown Hair.' Oh my, she was that lighthearted." Mrs. Guthro put her hand on the machine and fingered the broadcloth of Meg's riding skirt absent-mindedly.

"And did Calvin come after the dress next day?" Meg asked, eager to hear what part Marietta's brother played in the tale.

"Well, I finished up the dress that afternoon and then worked on the tablecloth and napkins I was hemming by hand to give her as a wedding present. I went to bed kind of late for me. Next morning I was just eating my breakfast when Calvin and his pa rode up, and I could see by their faces something was wrong. When had I last seen Marietta? they asked. I told them. Well, how did she seem? Was she worried? Had I seen any of the Donahues around? Then they told me. That morning they found a note on Marietta's dresser. She had eloped with Mike Donahue and please, would they ask John to forgive her!" Mrs. Guthro sighed and shook her head sadly. "And to this day we don't know why she did it. But I'm sure as I'm living that Mike Donahue forced her into it some way, although she has never breathed a word of it to anyone."

Meg let out her breath. "But John Parrish? What about him?"

"He arrived that day, Saturday, May 2. Calvin brought him over here in the afternoon. I spread the wedding dress out on the bed for him to see and told him all I knew. That poor, poor man! He just stood there looking down at all the lovely white satin and his eyes were full of tears. He showed me the fine wedding ring he had for her. Then he said something that was so beautiful I had him write it for me right here in the back of my Bible. Let me get it."

She took the book from the lower shelf of the table, opened it to the flyleaf, and put the Bible in Meg's lap. Written in a fine, shaded handwriting were two lines.

> Full many a flower is born to blush unseen,
> And waste its sweetness on the desert air.

Meg felt her eyes sting with tears as she read. "Oh, Mrs. Guthro, how true that is. Marietta's fine qualities certainly are wasted on Mike. I could see that from the first night I came." She closed the Bible and thought a moment. "Say, from what you have said, they must have been married a year ago today."

"That's right. Like as not Mike took her to town today to buy her some fancy, expensive doodad for the occasion. Just as if money could make up for all the misery he's put her through. Would you like to see the wedding dress?"

"You still have it?" Meg asked, surprised.

"Yes. I mentioned it to her once and I thought she was going to faint. 'Keep it,' she said. 'I never want to see it again.' So I've kept it. I asked Joyce once if I should give it to her mother, but she said no, it would only make her mother feel worse. Mrs. Lenfesty just went all to pieces for a few months until Marietta started going over there about every day. Joyce said she never explained a thing to her family, but having her visit seemed to comfort her mother. From little things Joyce has said now and then, I think Joyce is sort of taken with your cousin Todd. But the Lenfestys are mighty careful that she's kept out of his way. One daughter caught in the Donahue trap is enough."

"Oh, but Todd's different. You shouldn't even speak of him in the same breath with Mike," Meg said, coming to Todd's defense.

"Like as not," Mrs. Guthro agreed as she walked to a chest in the corner. "But still—once burned, folks are wary of the fire, you know." She lifted the lid, removed a sheet, then lifted out a white satin dress and held it up for Meg to see.

"Oh, my! It's lovely!" Meg touched it gently.

"Well, you should 'a' seen it on *her*. With her hoops holding out the skirt, her pretty neck above this bodice, and her brown curls over the shoulder! Oh, my! What a picture she was!" Mrs. Guthro folded the dress and returned it to the chest.

The clock above the fireplace began to strike. Meg glanced

at the time. "Eleven already? Why the time has just flown. I must start back. Thank you very much, Mrs. Guthro, for telling me all this."

"Well, everybody else around here knows, so I see no reason why you shouldn't. But living right there at Sycamore Park, if you should ever find out why Marietta became Mrs. Mike Donahue, I'd appreciate your telling me. You come back any time after next Tuesday to try this on again. I'll try to have a dress or two basted up by then too." Mrs. Guthro bade Meg good-by and watched her walk out to River Road.

As she walked along the edge of the ditch, Meg's head was full of the story she had just heard. The sun was warm on her head and the breeze blew her hair across her cheek. What a romance, that of Marietta and the handsome stranger from Kentucky! But what an ending, what an ending! Married to the despicable Mike!

VIII
DONATI'S COMET

Meg had so much to think about that she came to the rail fence at the edge of the Donahue cornfields before she realized she was near it. She held up her skirts and jumped the ditch neatly. She climbed to the top rail and sat there, one hand on the corner where the rails crossed, the other on the rail upon which she sat.

Just a year ago today Marietta had tried on her wedding dress and then a year ago tonight had eloped with Mike, Meg mused. How could she? Meg looked up at the blue sky, then down at the green budding bushes by the fence. What a puzzle! Spring was the very sign and promise of romance and love. It had brought tragedy to Marietta.

Meg heard the rattle of an approaching wagon. Hurriedly she put a leg over the top rail to climb to the other side of the fence. In her haste she failed to clear her skirts and they became entangled at the corner where the rails crossed. She stood on the middle rail, her skirts caught at the top. She pulled and tugged. The noise of the wagon ceased.

"Hold on there! I'll help you!"

She looked up and saw Calvin hop over the front wheel and jump the ditch.

"I'm caught," she told him, and felt her face redden with embarrassment.

"So I see." Calvin smiled slightly. "Step closer to the corner of the fence there, then your skirt will loosen and I can get it off the rail."

Meg complied and her skirts were released. Standing on the ground once more, she looked across the rails at Calvin. "Thank you very much. I don't seem to know much about climbing fences," she said with a laugh. "Did you get through last night all right with—with—your express?"

Calvin nodded. "Yes. Our packages are far from here now. I can't imagine what kept us from being chased. I was almost sure they were on our heels when we met you and Sis yesterday afternoon."

"They were." Meg brushed a splinter from the rail off her hand. "When we got to Sycamore Park, the sheriff and Mr. Cornell were eating supper with Uncle Barney and the others."

"Well, how come then——?"

Meg lifted her head and grinned at Calvin. "Marietta and I set up a campaign to keep them there as long as possible."

Calvin nodded. "You must have been successful. Otherwise they would have caught up with us long before we got to Ike's."

"The weather helped. The big storm persuaded them to spend the night." Meg wished this conversation did not have to end. But she couldn't keep him standing here at the fence much longer.

"By the way, what are you doing way over here?" Calvin asked. "Just walking about to inspect the Donahue acres?"

"No. I've been to Mrs. Guthro's to try on some things she's making for me."

Calvin looked toward the road at his wagon. "How about me taking you home?"

Meg brightened and felt her heart beat a little faster. "It would be out of your way and I'm sure you have things to do at your place."

"They can wait. Here, give me your hand, I'll help you over. Don't want you to get caught again."

Meg gave him a hand and climbed back over the fence. When she jumped the ditch, she felt as though she were floating over. The spring day seemed even more beautiful than before, when she sat beside Calvin in the wagon.

"What's Marietta doing this morning?" he asked.

"I didn't see her. She and Mike had gone to town by the time I was up." Meg pulled her feet under her skirts to keep Millie's boots hidden, though she supposed Calvin already had noticed them when her skirts were caught on the fence.

"Is she—is she all right? Was Mike nasty to her when she got home so late last night?" he asked with concern.

Meg hesitated. Should she tell him about last night in the parlor and that she knew about John Parrish? She looked across at his face turned toward the road ahead. The sunlight showed a short stubble of beard on his prominent jaw. His eyes were slightly squinted under the brim of his black felt hat. Suddenly she felt she had to tell him. He should know the kind of life his sister was leading in the big house.

She began by saying that Mrs. Guthro had told her this morning about the circumstances surrounding the marriage of Mike and Marietta. Calvin shook his head gravely as she described the way Mike had harrassed Marietta last night.

"I don't see how she puts up with him," Meg added. "He may be my cousin, but he's the meanest man I've ever met."

"You don't know the half of it," Calvin returned bitterly. "And to think my sister is married to such a devil and I can't do a thing about it." He pulled on a rein and turned off River Road and onto the Pike.

"I'm to have my first riding lesson this afternoon," Meg said, deciding it might be good to change the subject.

Calvin looked across at her. "So? Never ridden before?"

"No. Never even been on a horse. Todd is going to teach me."

Calvin frowned. "Just what is your opinion of Todd?" he asked.

"I like him very much. He seems to be cut out of a different cloth than the others. He's been very nice to me and he's considerate of Marietta too," she added.

Calvin pursed his lips firmly. "Still and all, he's a Donahue. You can't gainsay that."

"For that matter, so am I," Meg said vehemently.

He looked at her appraisingly. "I had forgotten," he confessed, "so I guess there are Donahues and Donahues. Some are of the devil's breed and some are—are——" He laughed. "I was going to say angelic, but I don't see any wings sprouting on you and I reckon angels don't wear boots."

Meg blushed. "They're Millie's," she explained, "and it was so wet and muddy——"

"Country girls often wear boots. Sensible thing to do. You and Marietta be at church tomorrow?" he asked.

"I suppose so. We've gone every Sunday since I've been here. But I haven't seen you there," Meg replied.

"Well, I might be there tomorrow."

Meg saw the jockey house come into view and wished that the big house were miles and miles farther than it was. She mentioned that Adelaide had started housecleaning at the jockey house this morning and how Tilda had compared her to a man-eating tiger where housecleaning was concerned.

"Yes, I've heard Adelaide Donahue is kind of a tartar. How is she toward Marietta?"

"Sort of cross and critical, but not mean. I think she resents another woman in the house who might take over her authority." Meg swayed with the roll of the wagon.

"Does she treat you well?"

"Yes, although she told me right off that it had not been her idea to give me a home." Meg noticed that Calvin had deep-set eyes like Marietta's.

He gave his attention to the horse and pulled slightly on the reins. The horse slowed to a walk. "Listen, Meg, why don't you plan to come to dinner with us after church tomorrow. Joyce has mentioned wanting you to come. I'll speak to Ma when I get home."

"With Marietta?"

Calvin frowned. "No. She hasn't had a meal with us since she married. Mike's orders, I guess. But there's no reason why you can't come, is there?"

"I guess not. But how will I get back to Sycamore Park?"

"Oh, I'll see that you get back."

Meg wished that one of her new dresses was made up to wear tomorrow. Well, anyway she could wear her new bonnet. She smiled at Calvin. "I'll look forward to visiting with Joyce and getting better acquainted with your family."

Calvin put one foot on the dashboard and held the reins loosely while the horse sauntered along leisurely. "Have you seen Donati's comet yet?"

"Only once. But it hasn't been visible very long. These last few months, with Grandma sick and all, I wasn't thinking much about the sky."

"Perhaps I can show it to you some night," he said. "You know some people are saying that the appearance of Donati's comet is a sign that a new leader is about to put in his appearance on this earth. Of course, it's just an old wives' tale, but we sure could use a good man in this country. I keep wondering how it's going to end, half our states free and the other half slave. I hope that comet *does* foretell the coming of a good man. How we need him!"

"Sort of like the star of Bethlehem, you mean?" Meg asked, thinking how pleasant it was to have Calvin talk to her like this.

"Well, you might say so. Of course, if folks really followed the teachings of the man who fulfilled the promise of Bethlehem's star, there'd be no need of a new leader now. 'Do unto others as you would be done by' never seems to be applied to dealings with black folks. We need somebody to hit slavery hard."

"Mrs. Stowe hit it hard in her book," Meg put in.

"Didn't she just!" Calvin exclaimed. "Her book has alerted people all over the world to what's going on in this country. If we ever do get that leader, she has paved the way for him in grand style."

"Did you know the play, *Uncle Tom's Cabin,* is going to be in Rollins two weeks from today?" Meg asked.

"Yes, I heard something about it."

"Marietta said we would be going," Meg informed him.

"Expect our family will too. Well, we're about to the Donahue lane. You know," Calvin said, looking directly at her, "I'm *glad* you got your skirts caught on the fence. Otherwise you might have been gone by the time I got there and we would have missed this chance to get acquainted."

"I'm glad too," Meg murmured.

Calvin pulled up at the entrance to the lane. "I'll let you out here. I don't go on Donahue land. No use stirring up trouble. Marietta's got enough to contend with. Just a minute. Stay right there. I'll come around and help you down."

He came to Meg's side of the wagon. She stepped over the wheel and put one foot on the hub. Calvin reached up, and before she could take his hand he had lifted her to the ground.

"Oh, thank you, Calvin. You are very strong."

Calvin grinned and pushed back his hat. "And you are as light as a feather. Nothing to you but skirts," he laughed, then added, "and boots."

Meg wrinkled her nose at him. "Thanks for the ride. I'll look for you in church."

Calvin stood for a time watching her walk toward the house. Then he got back in the wagon and turned it around. When Meg heard it rattling away, she faced the Pike and watched until the horse and wagon disappeared over the horizon.

Slowly she walked on. At the front of the house she took the path that led to the rear, pausing at the lilac bush to pick a sprig of the lavender blossoms and put them in her hair. She would go to the kitchen, return Millie's boots, and get her shoes and slippers. What a perfect morning it had been! Perfect, perfect, perfect!

At the dinner table Todd reminded her that the paddock was dry. So at half-past one she made her way, with unwilling steps, to the stables, both pockets of her dress filled with sugar to sweeten Blackie's disposition.

On the other side of the stables she found her horse already saddled and tied to the fence inside the paddock. Todd was not in sight. She approached the animal. He put his head over the fence and whinnied.

"So," she said, in a special tone she had been using to him, "you know me. Well, it's about time, because you and I have some special adventures ahead of us, Blackie boy. Here, I've brought you something good."

She reached into a pocket, then held an open palm under his mouth. His soft muzzle took the sugar. She fed him more, rubbing his nose with the other hand. "I'm not scared of your head any more," she murmured, "but I expect I'm going to be scared when I'm on your back. I hope you will treat me politely when I'm up there."

"Trying to bribe Blackie, I see," Todd said as he came up. "Well, it's good for him to know your touch and the sound of your voice. You make a fuss over him as often as you can. A dog can follow his master around and sit beside his chair. But it's the master who has to go to the horse to foster friendship between them. Here, come on inside the paddock."

Meg fed Blackie the rest of the sugar, then followed her cousin. He rolled a small keg near the left side of the horse and pointed to the saddle.

"You mount on the left side. Your right knee hooks over the horn, here." He pointed to the projection at the side of the pommel. "Your left foot is placed in this slipper-stirrup, as it's called. All right, climb on the keg and get on."

He gave Meg a hand and she stepped up. The horse shied to one side, then stepped back. Meg gritted her teeth, put her right hand on the pommel of the saddle, and got on. She hooked her right knee over the horn and Todd put her left foot in the one stirrup of the sidesaddle.

"Now the main thing," Todd told her, "is to keep an even balance. If you pull to one side you make it uncomfortable for your horse, and he'll get a sore back."

"And if he throws me, I may have more than a sore back," Meg said grimly.

"He won't throw you," Todd reassured her. "Now sit up straight. And remember that when I look at your back it must look exactly as though you were astride, except that there will be no leg on the right side."

He handed her the rein, explaining the pressure signals she must make to guide her horse. He took hold of her left foot. "The toes in the stirrup must be turned out a little, like this."

Looking up at his pupil, Todd led Blackie along the fence. "Don't wobble like that," he said quietly.

Meg felt as though she were perched high on a slippery roof, a roof that rose and fell under her like ocean waves. Back straight, center of the saddle, hands light on the rein, stirrup toes turned out, don't wobble; how could she remember it all?

For a moment she took her eyes from the horse's ears. On the other side of the fence she saw Chris and Ross grinning and nudging one another. Her eyes narrowed. They were probably betting on how soon she would fall off. She wouldn't!

Todd saw his brothers too. "Don't pay any attention to them, Meg. You are doing fine," he encouraged.

When the lesson was over and she had dismounted, Todd had her lead Blackie to his stall and showed her how to remove the saddle.

"There are always people out here to do this for you, but a good horsewoman must know how to saddle and unsaddle her mount. And a Donahue must be a good horsewoman." He smiled down at her.

Meg unstrapped the girth as directed. "Did you teach Marietta to ride or did she already know how when she came here?"

"Well, she knew how, but not well enough to suit Mike." Todd frowned as though remembering something unpleasant. "He gave her quite a lot of instruction."

"I can well imagine," Meg muttered. "Todd," she said on impulse, "I learned this morning all about John Parrish, how he was about to marry Marietta and how Mike eloped with her and all. What do you know about it?"

Todd didn't answer at once, but hung the saddle on the wall, then fastened the bar on Blackie's stall. He turned. "I'd rather not talk about it, Meg. You ask Marietta. She knows the particulars better than anyone."

Meg followed him outside. Joey led a horse toward them.

"Mr. Todd," the boy cried, "Fancy Boy just cut seven seconds off his record. If he keeps that up he'll be as good as Lexington, won't he?"

Todd hit the horse's rump affectionately. "Good for you,

Fancy. Take good care of him, Joey," he called as the horse and boy moved on.

"Who is Lexington?" Meg asked.

"A son of Boston and just about the fastest thing on the track. Made a record for four miles of seven minutes, nineteen and three-quarter seconds."

Meg tried to look impressed. "Boston," she repeated. "How queer to name a horse for a city."

Todd laughed. "Not for the city, but for the game of cards called boston."

"I guess you know everything there is to know about race horses."

"Not everything, but what *I* don't know, Pa and my brothers do. Ma used to say she thought I was born with a bridle in my hand."

"I'm going to have dinner with the Lenfestys tomorrow, after church," Meg informed him. "Calvin invited me. I'll be glad to get to know Joyce better. She is about my age, you know."

"Yes, I expect she is. I used to know Calvin and Joyce. We all went to the Four Corners school together several years ago. But I don't see much of them any more, at any rate not since——" He broke off.

At supper Mike pointed to the cameo brooch, matching earrings, and gold bracelet Marietta wore. They were his anniversary presents, he said, to remind her of the happy night of May 1, 1857, when she decided to elope with him.

Marrietta looked tired and pale. She ate very little and glanced at her husband beside her from time to time. What was she thinking? Meg wondered.

"I saw Calvin this morning," Meg said suddenly.

Ross put down his fork. "Was that slave-loving Lenfesty on our place?" he growled.

Meg observed the scowling faces of her cousins and uncle.

Only Todd was unperturbed at her statement. "He wasn't here. I met him on River Road after I'd been at Mrs. Guthro's, and he gave me a lift home. He let me out at the lane on the Pike. But why shouldn't he come here to his sister's home?" she asked courageously.

Marietta shook her head at Meg ever so slightly as Uncle Barney took a big bite of biscuit and replied with his mouth full.

"We don't want *anybody* snooping around our land, Meg, and that goes double for the Lenfestys, even if they are Marietta's folks. Maybe even *because* they're her folks." He gave Mike a knowing look.

"Well, they're nice people, and I'm going over there for dinner tomorrow after church," Meg stated firmly.

Adelaide glanced at her father, then at Marietta. "You going to let her go, Pa?"

Meg watched Uncle Barney butter another biscuit. "You forget, Addie, that Meg's one of us," he said with a wink in his niece's direction. "'Tain't likely she'll be tipping our hand to the Lenfestys. Go ahead, girl, and be sure to tell 'em about all the fine clothes your old uncle has bought you."

Meg saw Marietta's expression and wished she had kept still about the whole thing. Why, the way these people talked about the Lenfestys right before Marietta was awful!

Todd broke into the conversation, telling how well Meg had done at her first riding lesson.

"And why not?" Uncle Barney asked. "She's a Donahue."

After supper, Mike went into the hall toward the parlor, calling back for his wife to come on, he wanted her to play and sing for him.

Marietta paused long enough to whisper to Meg, "Was everything all right with Calvin?"

Meg pressed her arm. "Fine, just fine. Everything delivered as planned."

Marietta looked relieved and followed her husband.

Meg stayed behind, helped clear the table, and then went to the kitchen, preferring to talk with Tilda and Millie rather than watch her cousin intimidate his wife in the parlor. She helped dry the dishes and put them away. When there seemed nothing else she could do in the kitchen, she wandered out the back door.

Dusk was gone and stars were bright in the night sky. It was chilly and Meg folded her arms tightly for warmth.

She looked across the sky. Where was the comet Calvin had spoken of? Perhaps if she went on the other side of the house she could see it. She followed the gravel path around and stood just outside the sitting-room windows. She glanced in and saw Adelaide, knitting beside the lamp. Uncle Barney sat with his boots off, on the other side, reading a newspaper.

Faintly, from the parlor on the east side of the house, she could hear Marietta's voice and the organ. She walked away from the house and the light from the window. She wanted to be surrounded only by the night, away from the Donahues and their unsavory ways.

Out here it was clean and fresh. She looked up and there it was; Donati's comet with its tail blazing across the sky like a banner!

IX

SUNDAY AT CALVIN'S

Next morning Meg climbed into the buggy beside Marietta.

"The new bonnet is lovely on you, Meg," Marietta remarked as she slapped the reins and they proceeded toward the Pike on their way to church.

"I feel awfully dressed up in it. I never had one with pink flowers on it before. You don't think it too fancy for me, do you?"

Marietta shook her head. "No indeed. Blond hair, blue eyes, and pink cheeks were made for fancy bonnets."

"I wish you were going with me to your mother's after church," Meg said.

"Mike doesn't like to have me away at mealtime," Marietta said in a low voice. "But I'm glad Mama and Papa will have a chance to know you. And I want you and Joyce to be friends. Papa and Mama keep her pretty close."

Meg observed Marietta's profile and marveled at the length of her dark lashes. She wanted to ask her about John Parrish and why she had eloped with Mike. But there was a certain reserve in her cousin's wife that kept her from asking these intimate questions. So, instead, she spoke of her riding lesson, the clothes Mrs. Guthro was making, and Donati's comet.

This was the third Sunday Meg had attended the Mill Creek church with Marietta. They drove into the grove back of the church and Meg hopped out quickly and tied the horse.

"Well, thank you," Marietta exclaimed as she stepped from the buggy. "You wouldn't have done that three weeks ago. You would have been afraid of the horse."

"I know," Meg laughed. "Guess it's the Donahue way with horses coming out in me."

Many other carriages and buggies were in the grove. Here the horses would stand patiently, switching their tails, stomping, and trying to nibble the leaves on branches within reach, until the service was over.

In the churchyard Meg's eyes darted from group to group, hoping to see Calvin and his family. Mrs. Lenfesty approached, followed by Joyce, but Calvin was not in sight. Meg tried not to show her disappointment.

"Cal says you're going to have dinner with us," Joyce said. "I'm glad, Meg."

"Yes indeed. We are all happy to have you," Mrs. Lenfesty added. "Calvin will be a little late. A sick horse is delaying him." Mrs. Lenfesty's eyes twinkled. "It's been some time since Calvin showed an interest in church attendance. Strange the way a pretty girl can get a boy to do what his mother has been trying to accomplish for months." Mrs. Lenfesty turned to a group of men nearby and nodded to her husband. He joined her, spoke to Marietta and Meg, then left to round up the younger children, cavorting about with their friends.

Just as the church bell started ringing, Meg saw a buggy with its top folded back, come rolling at a high speed down the Pike. It turned into the church lane on two wheels and on back toward the grove. It was going fast, but not so fast that Meg couldn't recognize the driver. She smoothed her skirts and touched the ribbons of her bonnet with a gloved hand.

"You look fine," Marietta whispered, with a knowing smile as they followed the others toward the church.

Before they reached the door, Calvin ran up to join them. He slowed down, fell in step beside Marietta, and glanced across at Meg.

"Whew! Thought I wouldn't make it on time. Duke would choose this morning to have one of his spells. I've been up with him since a quarter to four."

"Cal has had Duke ever since the horse was foaled," Marietta explained to Meg. "How old were you when Papa gave him to you?"

Calvin took off his hat and wiped his brow with a handkerchief. "Let's see, Duke is twelve, so I was eight."

Meg did some mental arithmetic. Calvin must be twenty. She glanced at him quickly. He looked nice in his Sunday clothes, she thought. His face showed the ruddy glow of a close shave. His black coat, stretched snugly across his broad shoulders, had a faint smell of camphor. Meg smiled to herself and wondered how long it had been stored away.

Mrs. Lenfesty went into the family pew first, followed by the four children and Mr. Lenfesty. Joyce sat next to her father. Meg wasn't sure whether Calvin maneuvered it or not, but she found herself seated between him and Marietta. But no matter how it happened, she found it a very satisfactory arrangement to be holding a hymnbook with Calvin.

The service was a long one, but it didn't seem so to Meg. It was a good thing, she thought, that she didn't have to face Grandma afterward to answer questions about the sermon. That the sermon was against sin was all she could be certain of. She hoped God would forgive her for being so inattentive. She felt sure, though, that through the centuries He must have had to show special tolerance for all girls in love. She tried harder to listen to Reverend Renbarger's words.

After church she and Calvin walked with Marietta to the Donahue buggy. Calvin untied the horse while his sister climbed in.

"Now don't worry about Meg, Sis. I'll bring her home. It will be after dark, because I promised to show her the comet. It's quite a sight from the top of Wabash Hill."

Marietta smiled down at them. "I won't worry, Cal. Hope you enjoy the day, Meg."

"Oh, I shall," Meg answered.

Seated in Calvin's buggy, Meg felt as lighthearted as the singing red bird that flitted through the grove. Calvin untied his horse and jumped in beside her.

"Well, tell me," he said as he flourished the whip and the horse swung out onto the road, "how did the riding lesson go yesterday?"

Meg laughed. "I didn't fall off, but I think it will be some time before I venture out of the paddock."

"As soon as you feel equal to it, we'll ride together and I'll show you around this part of the county. Spring in Indiana is nice to look at, I think." He glanced at her. "You can go places on horseback where you can't take a buggy."

Meg nodded. She would ask Todd to give her another lesson tomorrow.

Down the Pike a way, Calvin turned off onto a narrower road. "No use getting home too soon," he said. "It'll be a while before Ma and Joyce have dinner ready. This road goes past our cherry orchard. It's kind of pretty right now."

The horse jogged along at an easy pace. Meg leaned back and folded her hands in her lap. May had never seemed so beautiful before.

"Tell me about Cincinnati," Calvin went on. "I've never been there. It must be quite a city."

Meg described her former home on the Ohio river. "Before Grandma got sick we used to take walks down to the river to watch the boats. It's quite a sight to see those big side-wheel steamers plowing through the water. Some of them carried passengers, others cargo from the South, mostly bales of cotton, of course."

"You know," Calvin said thoughtfully, "I sometimes wonder if our Northern states would be free states if our climate were good for cotton. Might not slavery have gotten a foothold here, just as in the South?" He looked at Meg and gave a slow smile. "That's one of my big problems; I see both sides of every question. Pa says I think too much. Of course, I'm positive that slavery is wrong, but I can see how hard it is going to be for those in the South to change their way of life; for I am sure that those poor colored folks have got to be set free."

"How do you think it can be done?" Meg asked.

"I don't know. But someone is bound to come along who will know. The good Lord is not going to allow so many of His people to live in bondage much longer. I tell you, Meg, some of the tales I hear from the poor devils I carry along north would just break your heart. Mrs. Stowe didn't tell the half of it."

There was silence save for the sound of the wheels and the horse's hoofs. Meg clasped her hands together tightly and wished this ride could go on and on. The cherry orchard, a vision of white blossoms, came into view.

"There it is." Calvin pointed with the whip. "Pretty, isn't it?"

"Lovely," Meg answered. "It looks like an orchard of winged snowflakes."

"It does at that."

Later, at the table, Meg sat between eleven-year-old Sarah and nine-year-old Betsy. All four of the younger children had asked to sit by her. Their mother had settled it by letting them draw straws, the two longest being the lucky ones.

Mr. Lenfesty bowed his head, the others lowered theirs, and quiet reigned as he said a simple grace. Then dishes were passed and the room was filled with the clink of china and silver.

Meg wondered again why Marietta had left this delightful family to live at Sycamore Park. After Mrs. Guthro's tale of John Parrish, she was sure it was not for love of Mike Donahue. Sarah passed her the noodles.

"Would you mind putting some noodles on my plate, Miss Donahue?" Betsy asked. "Sometimes big dishes are too heavy."

"Be glad to," Meg answered, dipping a generous serving on Betsy's plate. "But my name is Meg," she whispered as she handed the dish to Joyce, beyond Betsy.

Betsy smiled. "I know. Marietta told me you have a horse all your own. What's his name?"

"Blackie. As soon as I learn to ride well enough, I'll ride him over and you can see him. He's as black as midnight," Meg informed her.

"I guess they got about everything at Sycamore Park," Sarah put in. "Wish I could see inside that house, but Mama won't let——"

"Sarah, eat your dinner," her father interrupted.

"Yes, sir." Sarah picked up her fork.

"There are no Donahue children at Sycamore Park," Meg said, smiling across at twelve-year-old Peter and thirteen-year-old Nancy. "I'm the youngest Donahue there. And a family with children is much more interesting. Of course, there's Lizzie Ridenour, but I don't see her very often."

"Tell me, Meg," Mrs. Lenfesty said as she picked up the empty biscuit plate, "does Marietta eat properly? It has seemed to us that she is getting so thin."

"Well, I have noticed that Tilda tries to fix things to tempt her appetite, but Marietta doesn't seem to be interested in food."

Mrs. Lenfesty sighed and went to the kitchen for hot biscuits.

"Ma worries all the time about Marietta," Joyce said.

And well she might, Meg thought, remembering Mike's treatment of his wife.

"Marietta has been so kind to me," she said aloud. "I was pretty scared, I tell you, coming into a strange house."

Peter raised his head. "Anybody would be scared going there. Why, Jim Tatum told me that Old Man Donahue would just as soon scalp you as not and that even the horse thieves are scared of him and his sons."

"Peter!" Mr. Lenfesty exclaimed. "That will be enough!" He turned to Meg. "I'm sorry, Miss Donahue. Boys have a habit of talking out of turn."

"I'm sorry." Peter hung his head. "I forgot that you are their kinfolk."

"That's all right." Meg smiled gently at the boy. "I've been there long enough to learn that the Donahue name has a bad reputation around this neighborhood. But even so, I don't know what would have happened to me if Uncle Barney hadn't given me a home. He's very generous," she said, defending her uncle.

Calvin didn't say much during the meal, but Meg could feel his eyes upon her.

When they were finished, Joyce said, "Ma, you take a nap. Meg and I will wash the dishes."

"I'll do just that," Mrs. Lenfesty said. "Getting a family up and off to church is kind of chore. I'm sort of done in. Peter, you and Nancy fetch some more water from the well. I think the buckets are about empty."

"Yes, Ma," Peter replied.

Later, Joyce, her sleeves rolled up and her hands deep in soapsuds, chattered to Meg, asking questions about what went on at Sycamore Park.

Meg dried the dishes and thought what fun it was to do dishes with a girl her own age.

"Cal said Todd is teaching you to ride," Joyce remarked.

"Yes, he is. Todd is very nice—kind and considerate. He's the only one of my cousins I feel at ease with. He said he went to school with you and Calvin."

Joyce put a plate in the rinsing pan. "He did? I thought he had forgotten me, I haven't seen him for so long. Ma and Pa are suspicious of all the Donahues since Marietta eloped with Mike. They won't let me go to any parties if they think Todd might be there."

"I shouldn't think that likely. From what I have learned, the Donahues aren't welcomed or invited anyplace. But your parents shouldn't hold it against Todd that his name is Donahue. He has behaved like a real gentleman to me."

Joyce sighed. "I wish you'd tell them that. Marietta has, but I guess they think he just seems nice to her because anyone would be better than Mike. Ugh! I don't see how she stands him."

"Nor I," Meg returned, putting a pile of plates in the cupboard. "I suppose you don't know why she did it either."

"None of us do. Has she told you about John Parrish?"

"No, but Mrs. Guthro did."

"Oh Meg, he was the handsomest, sweetest man you'd ever want to know. He adored the ground she walked on. And she was so in love with him!" Joyce shook her head. "It's past all understanding."

"It is that."

At that moment Calvin entered, dressed in his work clothes. "Got to go out and see how old Duke is coming along. What are you girls going to do this afternoon?"

"Well, for one thing, I want Meg to see how the pups have grown; then I thought I'd show her the photograph album, and we might pick violets along the river." Joyce wrung out the dishrag, stepped to the back door, and threw out the dishwater. "Do you have any other ideas?" she asked when she returned.

"No, I guess not." Calvin hesitated, twirled the hat in his

hand, and looked at Meg. "But, Meg, if you get tired of my talkative sister, why I'll be down at the barn."

Meg smiled at him. "Joyce and I get along fine."

After Calvin had gone Joyce said, "You know, Calvin has never paid much attention to a girl before. I believe he's quite taken with you, and I'm glad."

Meg hung a dish towel over a chair back and felt her face grow warm. "He's very nice." She tried to make her voice non-committal. "In fact, you all are. It must be fun to have a large family."

"Well, as families go, ours is not so large, only eight since Marietta left. It must be good at Sycamore Park with hired help to do the work." Joyce took a broom from the pantry and swept the kitchen.

"Oh, I don't know. Many times since I came I've wished Uncle Barney were just a hard-working farmer with young children. That's the way I had pictured it. If it weren't for Marietta and Todd, I'd be pretty unhappy over there." Meg took the clean knives and forks from the table and put them in a drawer in the cupboard.

Joyce paused and leaned on the broom. "How I'd love to see the inside of that house!"

"Maybe Marietta and I can arrange a visit for you."

"No. I'm sure Ma wouldn't let me."

It was a full afternoon. Joyce showed Meg all over the rambling farmhouse, even the attic and the cool, apple-scented cellar. At the barn the pups were scampering up and down the slope that led up to the wide barn door. They yelped, nipped at one another, rolled over, and wagged their tails, eager to prove to the world that they were real dogs.

Joyce picked one up and handed it to Meg. "Feel how soft, Meg. Would you like to have one?"

Meg took the pup and stroked its head. "I'd be afraid Uncle

Barney's dogs would eat it up, they're so big; and they seem fierce, although I have made friends with one or two. I guess dogs are like people, if you speak to them in a friendly tone, like as not they'll quit growling."

Calvin was not in the barn.

"Duke must have been well enough to take to the pasture," Joyce said. "Want to go down by the river?"

Meg nodded, wondering if they would pass Duke's pasture on the way. Calvin might be there.

But the path to the river led through the woods. On the river bank violets bloomed profusely, sticking their purple heads above green leaves, as though inviting the girls to pluck them. Meg looked up and down the river, admiring the tall sycamores and bending willows on either bank.

"How beautiful," she said. "What river is this?"

"The Mississinewa," Joyce answered.

"Hmm. Nice-sounding name. Indian?"

"Yes. Lots of Indian fighting went on around here. You can find arrowheads most anyplace you look," Joyce replied.

"The Indian village isn't far, is it?"

"No. In fact, I used to pass it when I went to school, and I was scared to death of the barking dogs."

"Are the Indians unfriendly?"

"No. But when they are drunk they can be frightening."

"Yes, I know," Meg said, remembering racing day at Sycamore Park.

The girls picked large bunches of the long-stemmed violets, chattering all the while. Meg described the dresses Mrs. Guthro was making for her. Joyce told of the new dress she was making for herself. Meg asked if she were going to see the Uncle Tom show on the fifteenth. Joyce wasn't sure. Pa thought they all should go, but Ma was undecided.

Looking up at the sky, Joyce exclaimed, "Say, we've got to get home. Peter will be bringing the cows in to be milked."

"Do you know how to milk?" Meg asked.

"Of course. Don't you?"

Meg shook her head. "I'm afraid not. Suppose I could learn?"

"I'm sure of it. Come along, we must hurry."

The young Lenfestys laughed at Meg's attempts at milking. Even the cow turned its head and gave a disparaging moo.

Meg stood up. "I just can't make the milk come," she said. "And it looks so easy too."

"Never mind," Mr. Lenfesty said comfortingly. "Most folks don't get the hang of it the first time."

"That's right," Calvin put in. "Remember what a time you had teaching Nancy?"

Nancy, her head pushed against a cow's flank, gave a grunt. "Wish now I'd never learned. Seems as though whenever I'm doing something I like, it's always milking time." She turned her head and looked at Meg. "You won't ever have to do the milking at Sycamore Park, so take my advice and don't learn."

Meg smiled. "But I want to learn to do useful things." After all, she thought to herself, she might not always be living at Sycamore Park.

After supper Nancy and Sarah did the dishes. The others went into the parlor, where Joyce sat at the organ and the others sang the hymns she played. Meg thought Calvin had a fine bass voice.

At half-past seven Meg said she thought she should go home. She tried to tell Mrs. Lenfesty how much she had enjoyed the day.

"We are glad you came, dear," the lady replied. "It means a great deal to all of us to know you. And it's a comfort to me to have you there with Marietta. Your companionship will help her adjust to her new life in that household. The good Lord must have sent you." She gave Meg a gentle embrace. Meg noticed that there were tears in her eyes.

Outside, Calvin was waiting in his buggy. The family waved good-by from the porch as they drove away, Joyce calling out for her to return soon.

Calvin drove at a fast pace until they were out of sight, then he pulled the horse to a walk. "No need to hurry," he said. "It will be half an hour or so before we can see the comet."

"It's been a wonderful day, Calvin," Meg said. "You are lucky to have such a fine family."

"I know it. Hope you can come again, soon."

"I wish I could invite all of you to Sycamore Park, but——"

"I understand. Remember our Marietta has lived there a year and not one of us has set foot on the place." Calvin looked off toward the darkening horizon. "It's sad for my folks; they had such high hopes for Marietta. Ma had planned how she would visit her when she got settled in her new home in Kentucky. John Parrish was well liked by our whole family. I often wonder what has become of him."

"Well, according to Mr. Cornell, that planter, he's still living down there in Kentucky. But it was a wonder he didn't die of a broken heart," Meg said sentimentally.

"Not him. He was a strong man, able to live with disappointment. I imagine he'll marry and raise a good family. Tragedy often strengthens a person's spirit, if he's got the right stuff in him. And John Parrish certainly was made of good stuff. But I doubt if he'll ever be able to forget Marietta." Calvin sighed.

"Oh, look, there's the first star." Meg pointed.

"So it is. I've always liked this time of evening," Calvin said in a low voice. "Like to watch the dark-gray sky turn to the blue-purple of night. And the way the stars come into sight gradually, well, it's like as if they were curious and had come close to the sky curtain to look through and see what was happening down here. They must be disappointed at some of the sights."

"Why, Calvin, you talk like a poet!"

Calvin laughed. "Suppose you thought an Indiana farmer thought of nothing but raising corn and the price of hogs."

"No. I don't think I have thought of you as a farmer at all." Meg watched another star appear.

"But you have thought of me?"

Meg didn't answer at once. "Well, yes, on occasion."

"Good. We'll leave it at that. Mustn't press my luck. Look, there it is!"

Calvin pointed toward the sky, now scintillating with stars. The comet appeared among them like a fiery horse, its flaming tail streaming out behind as though it were galloping through the universe in a race with infinity.

Although Meg had seen the sight before, it seemed that here with Calvin she was watching it for the first time. Neither spoke for a while.

"Beautiful, beautiful," Meg whispered at last. "It must have some special meaning for all of us, just as you mentioned."

"Well, it's not hard to believe in a sign such as that one. Let's hope whoever is coming in its wake is equal to the job we've got waiting for him in this country."

At the lane that led into Sycamore Park, Calvin tied his horse to a fence post. "I'll not drive on Donahue land," he said, "but I'll walk you up to the house."

They walked past the race track and toward the house. They could hear the dogs barking at the stables on the other side of the track. The wind rattled the branches of the sycamores along the creek beyond. Meg drew her shawl closer and wondered if she could ever be happier than she was at this moment.

"This *is* a fine place," Calvin said as they approached the house, lights shining from its many windows. "You can't see all this from the road. Sis got herself a fine house, anyway, I'd say, even if her husband is a——" He broke off. "I'm sorry. That slipped out, Meg."

"Anything bad you want to say about my cousin Mike is true. Don't apologize." Meg stood at the bottom of the porch steps. "I wish I could ask you in, but——"

"That's all right. I wouldn't want to tangle with the Donahues. It would just make things worse for Sis. Well, good night and I'll see you again soon, I hope."

"I'll be at church next Sunday," Meg reminded him. She held out her hand. "And thank you for showing me the comet. I'll never forget this night."

"Nor I," said Calvin, holding her hand briefly.

Then he was gone and Meg was left alone with the night, Donati's comet, and a pounding heart.

X

THE UNCLE TOM SHOW

The following week Todd was surprised at Meg's enthusiasm for riding lessons. Each morning and afternoon found her on Blackie's back riding around and around the paddock.

Early Tuesday afternoon after her lesson, she walked to Mrs. Guthro's. It was good to walk, to stretch her sore muscles. Learning to ride was painful, even if one did manage not to fall off.

The riding habit was finished and two dresses were ready for first fittings. Going home, Meg carried the skirt and jacket over her arm. She walked slowly beside the orchard to enjoy the fragrance and beauty of the blossoms.

The blooms along the path were pale pink. Must be apple trees, she thought. Petals fell when the wind blew and settled like delicate snowflakes on the purple riding habit.

Meg brushed them off and smiled as she thought of herself dressed in the riding clothes, the beaver hat cocked at an angle, its white plume curled down fetchingly on her neck, and herself mounted on high-stepping Blackie. Well, just as soon as she felt she could manage her horse and stay on, she would ride to the Lenfestys'. She could fairly see Calvin's admiring glances.

This flight of fancy carried her to the end of the orchard at the edge of a cornfield. She hesitated. Should she go back the way she had come, or try to find her way along this side of the orchard? She decided on the latter course, for she wanted to explore all the areas of Sycamore Park.

A meadow lark trilled on its flight above the cornfield and a crow cawed a raucous reply. Meg breathed deeply. How good to be alive and almost seventeen on a May day!

Suddenly ahead, where the field dipped toward the creek, Meg saw a cabin. She stopped. Did someone live there? Perhaps some of the many hired men her uncle employed? Tilda had said that all the help lived at the jockey house, except a few grooms who had quarters in the stables. There was no smoke coming from the chimney and no one was about. Curious, Meg walked around to the front of the building.

The cabin itself was old and weathered, but the front door was made of new boards and fastened with a big lock. She approached a window, but brown paper covered the glass from inside, preventing any view of the interior. Whatever was in there, Meg decided, the owner wanted concealed; and the owner was, of course, Uncle Barney. What could be in there? She examined the other windows, but found them covered too. From what she knew of her uncle, she suspected that this cabin hid a dishonest project of some kind. However, she might be jumping to conclusions. It could be just a storehouse. She mustn't misjudge Uncle Barney. But isolated as it was, the cabin would be an ideal place for a shady activity.

Back in her room Meg spread the riding habit on the bed. What an artist Mrs. Guthro was, Meg thought, as she examined the seams of the jacket. It was still half an hour before supper, so she removed her dress and tried on the purple skirt and jacket.

As she stood before her mirror, there was a tap at the door. Marietta came in at Meg's bidding.

"So, she had it finished for you," Marietta said, rubbing a hand across Meg's shoulder. "It fits beautifully. Wait a minute, I'll get the hat."

She returned, the white-feathered beaver in one hand and a white satin stock for the neck in the other. She put the hat on the bed. "Here, put this stock about your neck. It will fit high around your throat, and the white satin against the purple makes a nice contrast. That's it. Now the hat."

Meg pulled the stock snug around her neck, then set the hat on her blond hair.

"A little more to one side," Marietta directed. "Meg Donahue, you are absolutely devastating!"

The mirror told Meg that the effect was flattering even beyond her own expectations.

"It's a lovely hat. Are you sure, Marietta, that you want to lend it to me?"

"I'm giving it to you. After I got it I knew that it did not become me. Come on downstairs. I want Tilda and Millie to see you." Marietta opened the door.

"You are going to make me vain as a peacock," Meg said as they reached the stairs. "Now if I can just manage to stick on my horse and not disgrace this outfit."

Meg was halfway down the stairs when she discovered that she had an audience below: Uncle Barney, Adelaide, Ben, and Todd.

Ben whistled and said, "Well, look at Cousin Meg, will you! A regular high-toned lady, if I ever saw one."

Uncle Barney's eyes gleamed. "Who says a Donahue can't look like a thoroughbred?"

"Hope I can act like one, Uncle Barney," Meg said as she reached the bottom step.

Adelaide looked her over critically. "The riding habit becomes you, Meg," she said at last.

"But can she ride?" Ben asked. "Fine clothes don't guarantee a good horsewoman."

"Don't worry about Meg," Todd said. "She's doing fine. By the end of the week she'll be out of the paddock."

Todd didn't compliment her costume, but his eyes told her that he was pleased with her appearance. In the kitchen Tilda and Millie were equally admiring.

On Friday Todd said she was ready to leave the paddock, so the two of them rode by the orchards, along the edge of the fields, and around to the creek. Meg's body was becoming used to the movement, and the muscular pain had eased somewhat, although occasional twinges told her that she was still a novice in the saddle.

"When are you going to wear your new riding clothes?" Todd asked.

"As soon as I'm sure I won't fall off."

"Don't you feel sure of yourself now?"

"Sure of myself, but not of Blackie. Who knows what he'll do? I certainly don't."

"I don't think he'll give you any trouble."

"Todd, what is that cabin over there used for?" Meg asked, pointing to the building she had observed before.

"Well, that used to be Pa's Trading Post when he first came here." They rode nearer. "Mike and Ross have been working over here. I don't know what they're up to. Well, I see they put up a new door. Got it locked too. I must ask Mike what he's got in there."

When they got back to the stables, Jethro came out as Meg dismounted. "Well, young lady, I 'spect you'll be riding hither and yon now. You learned real easy. I'll unsaddle for you."

"I still have a lot to learn, Jethro," Meg told him.

"Cousin Meg, the lessons are over." Todd unsaddled his own horse. "From now on it's up to you and Blackie. You know all the rules; all you have to do is ride and use them."

"You mean I can saddle up and ride whenever I want to?"

"Sure. And I expect Meg Donahue to become the best horsewoman for miles around." Todd grinned at her. "Practice makes perfect, you know."

The next day, after breakfast, Marietta said, "Meg, I'm riding over home. Want to come along?"

"Do you think I'm ready to ride that far?"

"Todd thinks so. Put on the new riding habit. I want Mama to see it."

As Meg dressed she hoped that Mrs. Lenfesty would not be the only one at home to welcome them.

They went by the way of the Pike, although Marietta said it was shorter across the fields, but there were fences to be jumped and Meg wasn't ready for that yet.

They stopped at the tollgate and visited with Mrs. Eakins. She told them an item of news: Dan Cochran was going to run for sheriff next fall against the present sheriff, Alf Ramsey.

"Oh, Mr. Ramsey is the one who stayed overnight, isn't he?" Meg asked.

Marietta nodded.

Mrs. Eakins pursed her lips. "Plenty of people in the county aren't satisfied with Alf's ideas of law and order. He closes his eyes to too much that goes on around here. Wouldn't surprise me a bit if Dan didn't beat him."

At the Lenfestys' the girls dismounted and tied their horses to fence posts near the barn-lot gate. Meg patted Blackie's nose and whispered, "Thanks for behaving so well."

Mrs. Lenfesty and Joyce were properly impressed with Meg's

habit. Joyce made her walk to the end of the hall and back again so she could get the full effect.

"Meg, you look beautiful! Oh, I wish my hair were blond! Doesn't she look as though she had stepped right out of *Godey's Lady's Book?*" Joyce clasped her hands.

Mrs. Lenfesty went back to the kitchen to continue with the churning. The girls followed. Joyce returned to her breadmaking. Meg and Marietta sat by the window.

Marietta pulled off her gloves. "Mama, I'd like to buy material for a riding habit for Joyce. What color do you think would be suitable?"

Mrs. Lenfesty stopped the up-and-down motion of the churn's dasher. "Marietta, we've been through this before. We cannot accept anything from you. You know how your father feels about Donahue money."

"But, Mama——"

"No, dear. Let's not speak of it."

Meg watched Marietta's face turn pale. Meg looked down at her own fine purple broadcloth jacket, purchased with Donahue money.

Mrs. Lenfesty brought the dasher into motion again. "We have decided to take all the children to see *Uncle Tom's Cabin* next Saturday," she said, trying not to notice her daughter's pained expression.

Marietta forced a smile. "I'm glad. Betsy has never been to the theater, has she?"

"No, and she is so excited. Anyone from your place going?" Mrs. Lenfesty asked.

"Todd is taking Meg, Adelaide, and me," Marietta replied. "Mike and the others aren't interested, they said."

Meg and Marietta stayed for more than an hour, while Joyce made the dough into loaves and put them in a warm corner to rise, and Mrs. Lenfesty took the butter from the churn, put it into a wooden bowl, worked it with a butter paddle, and drained off the last drops of the buttermilk. After salting it, she scraped the golden mass into a brown crock.

"How about a glass of fresh buttermilk, Meg?" she asked, as she poured the white liquid from the churn.

"Yes, thank you." Meg drank the buttermilk slowly, enjoying the tart taste, and wondered if Calvin ever came in from the fields in the morning.

But now it was time to go, and still he had not appeared. Outside, Meg found Blackie neighing and pulling at his tether. A bantam rooster and a flock of hens were picking and scratching near the fence. Marietta untied her horse and mounted. Mrs. Lenfesty and Joyce stood outside the kitchen door, watching.

Meg untied Blackie. The horse tossed his head and sidled toward the fence. Meg put her left foot in the slipper-stirrup, as Todd had taught her, reached up, caught hold of the horn, and pulled herself to the saddle. Before she could get her right knee over the horn, the bantam rooster lifted his tiny red cockscomb and gave a loud COCK-A-DOODLE-DO directly under Blackie's nose. The horse, startled, reared and lifted his front feet off the ground momentarily, just long enough to cause his surprised rider to slide off his back and fall in a heap on the ground.

Marietta was off her horse at once; Joyce and Mrs. Lenfesty ran from the house, and Calvin came bounding out of the barn and down the slope.

By the time the four approached, Meg was on her feet, her hat on the back of her head, her purple skirt and jacket gray with dust.

"Meg, Meg, are you hurt?" Marietta cried.

Meg rubbed her elbow. "Not very much," she answered as she looked up at Calvin's concerned face. "But my pride is bruised. I wanted so much to show all of you how well I could ride. Grandma used to tell me that pride goeth before a fall.

How right she was." She managed a quick smile, straightened her hat, and began brushing her skirt.

Calvin took Blackie by the bridle and stroked the horse's neck to sooth him. "Anyone could have fallen off," he told her. "That blamed rooster scared your horse. I saw it all from the barn."

Joyce and Marietta helped brush Meg's skirt.

"Well now," Meg said, approaching the horse. "I'll try again."

"I'll hold his head until you get properly seated," Calvin said solicitously.

In the saddle Meg looked down at him. "Thank you, Calvin. I'm all right now. Let him go."

"Doesn't she look nice, Cal?" Joyce asked, standing near her brother.

"Yes, indeed. Now be careful, Meg," he admonished as he released the bridle. "Don't want you to break any bones."

Meg rode after Marietta, muttering to her horse. "Blackie Donahue! Of all the times for you to throw me, just when Calvin was looking at us. And I did so want him to see us at our best."

Saturday, May 15, was cool and clear. Tilda fixed an early supper for Marietta, Adelaide, Todd, and Meg, so that the four of them were on their way to town by a quarter to six.

Wearing her new light-green challis dress and flowered bonnet, Meg felt very grand seated in the back seat of the carriage with Marietta. She wondered if the Lenfestys would sit near them, so that Calvin might notice her new finery. After last Saturday's inglorious episode, she wanted him to see her tonight, dignified and well-attired.

She observed the back of Adelaide's bonnet and the small black plume on top that bobbed every time she moved her head. Todd sat erect beside his sister. Meg cast a side glance at Marietta, noting how sad her face was in repose. It seemed to Meg that the face had grown thinner during the past month. No wonder Mrs. Lenfesty was worried about her daughter.

Marietta, catching Meg's eyes upon her, smiled and touched Meg's arm. "You look lovely, Meg dear, just like a part of the green, blossoming spring that is all about us."

Todd glanced back. "She sure does. The Rollins boys will be knocking me down for an introduction to our cousin when we get to town."

"I'm not interested in the Rollins boys," Meg laughed.

Adelaide turned around. "You should be," she said sharply. "One old maid in the Donahue family is quite enough."

Meg was surprised at her cousin's tone. She had no idea that Adelaide resented her unmarried state.

"Adelaide," Marietta said with feeling, "there are worse things than being an old maid."

Adelaide didn't answer. Todd hunched his shoulders as though the conversation made him uncomfortable. He swung the whip from its socket and cracked it over the wheel. "Get along there, Bart and Bell! You want us to be late for the show?"

It was still light when Todd tied the team to the hitching rail at the courthouse. They crossed the dusty street and joined the many people walking toward the Daly Theater.

"It looks as though just about everybody in Rollins is going to the show," Todd remarked to the ladies.

"Well, the play being from such a famous book has something to do with it," Adelaide remarked. "People who wouldn't darken the door of a theater regard this as more of a sermon against slavery than a theatrical production."

"I don't see how they can get all of the book into a play," Meg said, holding up her skirts just enough to keep them out of the dust without showing her shoes above the instep. "You know, I've never been to a play put on by actors in a real theater."

Todd laughed. "Well, our theater wasn't built to be a theater in the beginning. Who was it that built it, Marietta?"

"It was called Daly Hall for years," Marietta answered, "and was built by Tad Daly for town meetings, political gatherings, and the like, Grandma told me. Then, when he died, his sons remodeled it and changed its name to Daly Theater. Grandma says calling it a theater keeps most church members from going there, even for things other than plays."

"Well, I believe there are lots of church members in this crowd," Adelaide said with a glance at those walking in front of her. "I see the Barley family up there, all of the children and even Grandma and Grandpa. They've been the pillars of the Methodist Church ever since its beginning days here. *Uncle Tom's Cabin* seems to be uniting saints and sinners, at least for tonight."

Todd bought the tickets. The prices were twenty-five cents for seats in the front half of the hall and ten cents toward the rear. Meg was impressed at the Donahue affluence which permitted Todd to spend a whole dollar for their evening's entertainment.

Meg's eyes grew wide as they passed through the door into the large hall filled with row after row of benches. Lamps hung at intervals along the whitewashed walls, lighting the place with flickering radiance. The first four rows were already filled, so Todd led them to places in the fifth. He laughed as he sat between Adelaide and Meg and remarked that ladies should buy two tickets, their skirts took up so much room.

Meg glanced around, hoping to catch sight of Calvin and his family. Marietta spotted them seated toward the rear, in the ten-cent seats.

Meg looked up at the stage with its concealing curtain, a

picture of green trees and a waterfall painted upon it. Across the stage, in front of the curtain, was a row of lamps, with tin reflectors fastened to their chimneys on the side toward the audience. These lamps, Marietta told her, would be lighted when the play started, so they could see the actors' faces clearly.

The theater was filling up fast. Todd pulled out his watch. "Only seventeen minutes now till it begins," he said.

Meg swallowed hard, her mouth dry with excitement. At half-past seven she saw two men walk along either side and turn down the lamp wicks until the hall was only faintly lighted. Then the two climbed to the stage and lighted the lamps there. The curtain grew bright in the reflected illumination.

As the audience became quiet, Meg clasped her hands tightly, not taking her eyes from the curtain. Slowly and jerkily it rose and she stepped into the dining room of the Shelbys on their plantation in Kentucky. There, in the flesh, were Eliza and her husband, George Harris, talking of their difficult lives as slaves.

The scene changed to the outside of Uncle Tom's cabin, with Uncle Tom learning that he had been sold down the river.

It wasn't a play to Meg, but the real thing. Poor Uncle Tom, forced to leave his wife and children; and brave Eliza, running across the ice on the river to save her little boy from the slave trader. Meg's handkerchief was soon wet with tears.

Audience tension was relieved somewhat by the appearance of Topsy and her wayward antics, but tears flowed again with the death of the golden-haired child, little Eva St. Clair.

Toward the end of the play Simon Legree was hissed at every entrance, and sometimes a voice in the audience called out an epithet at the villainous slave-beater. By the last scene Meg felt that she couldn't cry any more, her throat ached so.

Young George Shelby had come from Kentucky to buy back Uncle Tom from the cruel Simon Legree. But he was too late, Uncle Tom was dying.

George: Oh, Tom, you mustn't die! . . .

Tom: Massa George, dat's all pas' an' gone now. I's right at de doh, goin' into de glory. . . . Dere's Massa St. Clair an' li'l Eva. . . . I's comin'. . . . I's comin'. . . .

George: He's gone! Dear old Uncle Tom, your body shall rest beneath the blue grass of your beloved old Kentucky till the Judgment Day!

The curtain fell, the lamps in the hall were turned up, and the audience stumbled out into the night.

Meg forgot her new dress and bonnet and that Calvin was near. Only little Eva, Uncle Tom, and slavery were real.

XI

SEVENTEEN AT LAST

As time passed Meg grew more confident in her riding. Daily she rode Blackie on exploring expeditions around and through Sycamore Park. Once, in early June, she met Calvin on horseback, and he showed her a narrow trail to the river where some rocks formed a falls halfway across and the water splashed down in noisy confusion, with the sun shining through the spray in a rainbow of color.

Summer came and days were hot. Meg packed the riding habit away with camphor crystals to keep out the moths and wore a thinner dress for riding. Jethro put the summer chairs on the front porch and she found it pleasant to sit there and watch the activity around the stables and track below. Uncle Barney and his sons seldom stayed at the house long enough to sit on the front porch, but Adelaide and Marietta often joined her.

One evening Marietta asked when Meg would be seventeen. Meg replied, "June 24."

"Why, that's week after next," Marietta exclaimed. "Grandma asked only yesterday when I was in town. She wants to give a party for you."

"She does? I've never had a party given for me. In fact, I've only been to a very few." Meg leaned forward, her pulse quickening at the idea of a party for her, held in the big Lenfesty home in Rollins.

Adelaide rose suddenly, her hoops swaying with her quick movement. "You mean Mrs. C. Wadsworth Lenfesty would condescend to entertain for one of the Donahues?" she asked with a mirthless laugh. "If you are so anxious for Meg to have a party, why not have it here at Sycamore Park? Our house is as fine as your grandmother's."

"Adelaide, you know very well we couldn't," Marietta said gently. "We couldn't count on your father or the others to behave themselves. And not many parents would permit their young people to come here."

"And what makes you think they will let them go anywhere to a party given for a Donahue?" Adelaide asked bitterly as she disappeared into the house through the open door.

Meg felt uneasy. The picture of herself in her new party dress, the guest of honor at a gala affair in town, fell to pieces at Adelaide's question.

"Don't mind Adelaide," Marietta tried to reassure her. "Mama told me that when this house was first built, Father Donahue tried to give a party for Adelaide. It was a failure; scarcely anyone came. She has never forgotten the incident."

"But maybe she's right," Meg said in a low voice. "Maybe no one would come anywhere to a party for me."

Marietta touched Meg's hand. "Don't worry. No one in the county would ignore an invitation to a party at Grandma's."

Meg slapped a mosquito on her wrist and watched the fireflies twinkle on and off as they flitted through the dusk. "What do they do at one of your grandmother's parties?"

"Oh, they have music, play dancing games, sing, sometimes play charades, talk, and of course eat. Grandma always has good food in her dining room. You'll enjoy it, Meg, and the young people in the vicinity will get to know you."

"I wonder if they'll want to know me," Meg answered dubiously, shaken by Adelaide's outburst.

To the surprise of all and to Meg's dismay, Mike announced at the table the next week that *he* would escort his wife and cousin to the birthday party.

"What's the use of marrying a Lenfesty if I can't take advantage of it," he grinned maliciously. "I always wanted to attend one of those society shindigs Old Lady Lenfesty puts on. Now's my chance. Think I'll get me some new duds to wear too."

Meg watched Marietta at this announcement. The young wife's hand trembled and she put down her fork. "Of course, Mike," she said in a controlled voice. "Grandma will be glad for you to come."

"I doubt that," Mike answered. "This will be the first time you have been to a party there since before we were married. That last one I had to watch from the outside. Now this time it will be my turn to howl, and on the inside too!"

Something inside Meg shriveled as she watched Marietta. She knew Marietta was remembering that affair at her grandmother's, the one at which her engagement to John Parrish had been announced. What would Mike do at the birthday party? Probably spoil it.

Adelaide looked at Mike, her lips held in a disapproving line. "Mike Donahue, you're not to cut up any of your devilish didoes at Meg's party. Understand?"

Mike rose. "Don't fret yourself, Sister," he said mockingly. "I'll behave like a Kentucky gentleman." He hitched his gun belt up on his hips, put his hands in his pockets, and swaggered from the room.

"Marietta," Todd said, after Uncle Barney and his brothers

had left the table, "do you suppose you could get me an invitation to Meg's party? You may need some help with Mike before the evening is over."

"Of course, Todd. It will be good to have you there." Marietta sounded relieved.

Meg gave a short sigh. Perhaps Todd *could* keep Mike civilized for the evening.

Dawn found June 24 hot and sultry. Meg was wakened very early by two flies buzzing annoyingly over her face. She wanted to just lie there and enjoy being seventeen at last, but the flies persisted in their torment. She covered her face with the sheet and tried to imagine how she would look tonight in the blue silk dress she had not yet worn. Marietta had said Calvin would be there. Would he ask her to dance, and could she if he did? She had heard of the waltz, but had never seen it done. Once she had taken part in a Virginia reel, but that was the extent of her dancing.

It was hot under the sheet and she could still hear those dratted flies. She threw back the sheet, hopped out of bed, and stood at the open window, but there was no coolness in the heavy air that blew in. More flies buzzed in and out. A mourning dove cooed its sad notes from the maple tree, a rooster crowed, and cows mooed impatiently as they waited for hands to relieve their heavy udders. Morning had come again to Sycamore Park!

Meg wiped her moist forehead with the sleeve of her nightgown. What a scorcher of a day! She hoped it would be cooler by nightfall. She went about dressing without much enthusiasm. Tightly laced in stays, she put on three cotton petticoats and one of linen, then topped the lot with a gingham dress.

It was a quarter to six when she entered the kitchen. Tilda was stirring corn meal into a pot of boiling water.

"Well, happy birthday, Miss Meg. You got up early to celebrate, didn't you? Hot, ain't it?" Tilda put down the wooden spoon, picked up a corner of her apron, and wiped her moon-shaped face.

"It is for a fact," Meg answered as she took a cloth from a nail in the pantry. "Thought I'd get my dusting done before breakfast. It's bound to get hotter as the day wears on."

"You shouldn't be doing a thing on your birthday."

"Oh, I wouldn't want to slight my work. Where are Millie and Lizzie?"

"Picking peas in the garden. Trying to get it done before the sun gets any hotter." Tilda stepped to the table and used a large knife on a ham.

Dustrag in hand, Meg disappeared into the front of the house.

By noon the sun was so hot, Meg was sure it would have cooked an egg if she had broken one on the roof. She had little appetite for the fried-chicken dinner Tilda had cooked for her birthday, and she watched distastefully as the male Donahues stowed it away.

Todd said, "I think we better go into town early, for there's going to be a storm come evening or my name isn't Donahue. This heat has got to break."

Marietta turned to her husband. "Shall we start about five, Mike?"

"I suppose so. Wouldn't want a storm to spoil my new clothes. You wear that new jewelry I got you. I want folks to know that there's nothing cheap about Mike Donahue."

"Yes, Mike."

It was stifling in Meg's room that afternoon as she dressed. Outside the sky was cloudless and deep blue; the sun was a searing orange flame, and every now and then the rumble of distant thunder troubled Meg's ears.

Millie came in and helped fasten the dress down the back, saying as she did so, "This is a mighty nice dress. You'll be the prettiest girl there. My land, but you got a little waist! I could 'most nigh span it with my hands. Now just stand there a jiffy. I'm going to sponge your face and neck with cold water."

Refreshed by Millie's ministrations, Meg picked up a white silk bag, hung the drawstrings over her arm, and took one last look in her mirror. The pale-blue silk was exactly right, she decided, to set off her blond hair. And her waistline *was* small, justifying the tight lacing she had given her stays. Her skirt stood out over her hoops, and the festoons of Valenciennes lace gave it such elegance that it was hard for her to believe the reflection was Meg Donahue.

Millie patted her shoulder as she left. "You have a good time. I 'spect you'll remember this birthday when you're an old, old lady. It's quite a feather in your cap having old Mrs. Lenfesty give a party for you. Howsomever, I'd feel easier in my mind if Mike wasn't going. Even in all those fine new clothes he bought, he's the same hell-raisin' devil underneath. But don't you worry. He wouldn't dare start a rumpus at the Lenfestys'. Hope the storm holds up till you get home."

As Meg descended, her broad skirt very nearly filling the width of the staircase, she saw Marietta, Mike, and Todd waiting below.

Marietta, Meg thought, looked like a delicate rose, dressed in taffeta of such pale pink as almost to be mistaken for white. Mike, a cocky tilt to his head, grinned up at Meg, while Todd nodded in satisfaction.

"Well, well, Cousin Meg, you look like a high-stepping filly ready for a race," Mike shouted. Meg was afraid he had been drinking, his eyes were so bright. "Guess the upper crust in Rollins will have to take a back seat to the Donahues tonight," he added as he looked at his wife.

Mike himself was resplendent in tight-fitting gray trousers, long-tailed coat, and yellow satin vest. His black hair curled in damp ringlets on his moist forehead. If she hadn't known of his inner cruelty, Meg thought she would have considered him downright handsome. In contrast, Todd seemed almost somber in a black suit.

"Meg," Marietta said, proffering a small box, "here is a little present from all of us."

Taking the elongated box, Meg opened it and gave a little gasp of delight at the folding fan inside. She took it out, gave a little touch to the ivory handle, and the fan opened, showing hand-painted roses on white silk, tipped with very fine lace.

"Oh, how beautiful! I've never had anything so lovely. Thank you, thank you! You are too good to me. I don't deserve it." She hung the white silk cord of the handle on her wrist and held up her arm to admire the effect.

"Nothing's too good for a Donahue," Mike bragged. "Our women must have the best."

Outside, two carriages waited for them. Todd laughed and said they would never have gotten two hoop skirts in one carriage. Meg sat gingerly in the back seat of one, her dress spreading out on either side. Todd took off his coat, folded it, and put it beside him in front.

"Guess you won't mind a shirt-sleeved driver, will you, Meg? No use being so fancy till we get to town." He watched Mike and Marietta start off toward the Pike, Mike whipping his team and pulling on the reins until the horses reared and then bolted down the lane at high speed. "That fool, Mike! Does he want to kill his team? If he keeps that up they'll be in a lather by the time he gets to town."

The Pike was dusty. Todd slowed down so that the cloud Mike's horses raised could settle before he and Meg got to it. It was nearing six o'clock by the time they reached Rollins. The other Donahue carriage was hitched at the Lenfestys' front gate.

Todd drove around to the barn so that his horses could drink from the watering trough in the barn lot. He assisted Meg from the carriage and she entered the big house by the side door. The elder Mrs. Lenfesty greeted her and exclaimed over the beauty of her dress. Marietta, she said, had gone upstairs to rest before the party. She didn't know where Mike had gone, he had disappeared almost as soon as they had arrived.

Mrs. Lenfesty persuaded Meg to rest too. Walking through the house to the front hall, Meg noticed that most of the furniture had been removed and the rugs taken up. Upstairs in the room assigned to her, Meg removed her dress and hoops and reclined on the bed, but she was too excited to relax.

The sweet odor of lavender came from the pillow slip upon which her head rested, but the rattle of distant thunder offset any soothing effect the perfume might have had on Meg Donahue. At last she gave up and went to the window, which looked down on a side yard surrounded by an iron fence. It was a well-kept yard with closely cut grass, flower beds, and trees along the fence. There were benches and chairs and Japanese lanterns hung on wires between the trees. Evidently the party was expected to spread to the outdoors, Meg surmised.

At a quarter after seven Marietta, not looking at all rested, came in, lighted the candles, and fastened Meg's dress for her. They went down together.

By seven-thirty the street up and down in front of the Lenfestys' was filled with carriages, the horses stomping the dust and flicking their tails to shoo away the flies. Sunset brought no relief from the heavy air.

Meg stood at the front door with Marietta and her grandmother and was introduced to the guests as they entered. By the time Calvin and Joyce arrived it was dark and the numerous candles in the chandeliers of each room had been lighted, casting a soft glow over all.

Calvin leaned down and said seriously, "Many happy returns of the day, Meg."

"Thank you, Calvin," she returned, liking the light in his eyes.

One of the three fiddlers drew his bow across his fiddle and called out, "Line up for a Virginia reel."

"Will you do this reel with me?" Calvin asked.

"Yes, but I warn you I've only tried it once before."

Folding doors had been opened and three rooms formed a long dancing area. The young people lined up on two sides, the girls on one, their partners opposite. The fiddlers began the tune; the young people clapped their hands as they began to sing "Weevily Wheat," and the top and bottom couples began the figures.

> Come down this way with your weevily wheat,
> Come down this way with your barley,
> Come down this way with your weevily wheat,
> To bake a cake for Charley.
>
> O Charley, he's a nice young man,
> O Charley, he's a dandy,
> Charley hugs and kisses the girls,
> And feeds them all on candy.
>
> The higher up the cherry tree
> The riper grow the cherries,
> The more you hug and kiss the girls
> The sooner they will marry.

By the time she and Calvin were the bottom couple, Meg had watched enough of the others go through the pattern to be able to do the figures without difficulty. She forgot the heat, forgot to wonder what had happened to Mike, forgot Marietta sitting with the older women, forgot her blue silk dress which rippled and swayed with the movement of the hoops beneath. Real only were her tapping, stepping, rhythmic feet and Calvin's smile as he swung her at the end of each figure.

> It's swing oh swing with your weevily wheat,
> It's swing oh swing with your barley,
> It's swing oh swing with your weevily wheat,
> To bake a cake for Charley.

When the music stopped, Meg realized that Joyce had been in the reel too; her partner was a big farm boy from a nearby township. Meg looked around for Todd, but he was not in sight. What had happened to her two cousins?

The young people went outside to try to cool off before the next reel. Calvin took Meg to the well near the kitchen and drew up a bucket of cold water. She drank thirstily from the cup that hung at the well. She took a handkerchief from her bag, wiped her hot face, then unfolded her birthday gift and fanned herself.

Calvin looked up at the sky as he hung the cup back on its nail. "Guess we won't see our comet tonight," he said. "There'll probably be rain before morning. Good thing too; the corn needs it. Like to sit down and cool off for a spell?"

"Yes."

"There's a bench over there."

The bench was near the back of the house with the barn lot in view. Occasionally they could hear the horses, tied there, stomp and neigh, impatient to be home in their familiar stalls.

"I haven't seen you since that day at the river," Calvin said. "I couldn't get to church last Sunday. Had to work in the fields even if it was the Lord's day. The crops sort of got ahead of Pa and me."

"I missed you."

"That's nice to know." Calvin paused. "I thought Mike and Todd were going to be here."

"They brought us, but I haven't seen them since we arrived. Where do you suppose they are?"

"Knowing Mike, I'll wager he's someplace in town getting drunk."

"Oh, dear! Maybe Todd is out looking for him."

"Well, it will be better for Sis's sake if Mike Donahue doesn't show up here. The music is starting. Shall we go in and see what's doing?"

"Let's do." Meg got up, Mike and the coming storm forgotten.

At half-past eight the doors of the dining room were opened and Grandma Lenfesty's cooking art was displayed in all of its tempting varieties. Grandma and her hired girl had cooked all day for the affair, and young and old now attacked the food in full appreciation.

There was ham, chicken, bread and sweet butter, honey, three kinds of jelly, four kinds of pickles, green beans, peas, and tiny new potatoes swimming in a thick cream sauce; and then there was a table in the corner with raspberry, cherry, apple, custard, peach, and blueberry pies, and angel food, devil's food, marble, spice, and sponge cakes. The coffee in the cups was strong and hot and the milk in the glasses was heavy with cream.

Meg had been too excited to eat before she left Sycamore Park and now she sampled everything hungrily, wishing she had not laced so tightly and could take second helpings.

She and Calvin ate with another couple, Mary Keller and Oliver Wainwright, in the side yard, where not a breath stirred the leaves. The candles inside the paper lanterns cast an eerie light over the grounds. Meg shivered in spite of the heat.

The elder Mr. Lenfesty came outside and looked around, then approached Calvin.

"Cal," he said, "I'm sorry to interrupt, but may I see you inside for a minute?"

"Of course, Grandpa." Calvin excused himself and went inside.

Mary and Oliver returned to the dining room to replenish their plates. Meg said she couldn't hold another morsel. Calvin returned and sat down beside her.

"Meg," he said, his voice tinged with regret, "I've got to leave." He paused. "Some express has just arrived. And Grandpa wants it taken north before the party breaks up and folks go to the barn for their horses. Do you understand?"

"Of course."

"I wanted to take you home after the party, but now—— I was going to tell you how pretty you look——" Calvin hesitated.

Amid the mumbling conversation and the clinking of forks against china, a girl's laugh rang out. "That's all right, Calvin. I can go home with Todd," Meg said understandingly.

She stood at the well and watched Calvin's shadowy figure enter the barn lot, untie his team, back out the surrey, and wait until two indistinct forms crept from the darkness of the barn and climbed into the back of the vehicle. Calvin drove out the back way.

Meg got another drink from the bucket. Just as she hung up the cup, two gunshots rang out at the front of the house! Others followed in rapid succession!

Fright swept over her. Was it the sheriff coming to arrest Calvin for helping runaway slaves? She held up her hoops in front and ran around the house. Other guests were running to the front fence to discover the cause of the commotion.

Horses hitched along the street stomped, neighed, and pulled at their tethers in fright. Men on horseback galloped up and down, firing more shots into the air. There was a shot at the front gate and a man burst through, shouting. "I've come to dance with my wife! Where is she?"

In horror Meg saw Mike reel in, roaring drunk. Were those in the street more of her male cousins? Were the wild Donahues at it again? Where, oh where was Todd?

She followed Mike into the house and saw Grandpa Lenfesty take his arm and try to lead him away. But the towering Donahue shook the old man off as though he were a rabbit. Marietta came out of the dining room and looked at her husband in wide-eyed terror.

"Where are those fiddlers?" Mike yelled. "I've come to dance." He flourished his pistol and the frightened fiddlers put their plates on the mantel, took up their instruments, and began to play wildly.

Mike grabbed Marietta, his pistol still in hand, and whirled her around and around the room until Meg was sure the poor girl would faint. The other guests stood at the doors and windows, looking on in frightened fascination.

There was a blinding flash of lightning followed by a violent clap of thunder. The fiddlers did not halt and Mike's heavy boots clomped heavily as he swung Marietta off the floor like a limp doll.

Meg put her hand over her mouth to keep from screaming. What a relief to see Todd dash in through the hall.

He paused momentarily in the doorway, then ran to the couple and grabbed his brother by the shoulders.

"Mike, you fool! Stop it! Stop it!"

Mike flung Marietta from him and shook Todd from his back with ease. He fired a shot at the mirror over the mantel; the fiddlers fled at the ensuing crash.

He turned on Todd and yelled, "Nobody stops me, not even you, Todd Donahue!" He fired again and Todd fell. Mike picked up Marietta as if she were a fluttering bird and ran through the door and out the gate just as the skies opened up and let the rain down in a furious torrent.

Millie had spoken truly; Meg would remember her seventeenth birthday when she was an old, old lady; in fact, to her dying day!

XII

"A MAN NAMED LINCOLN"

It was still raining next morning when Meg wakened, lying
beside Joyce in one of Grandma Lenfesty's guest rooms. Neither
had slept well.

Last night some of the men had lifted Todd to a couch in
a back room, while others rode out into the storm to find Dr.
Dixon. Grandpa Lenfesty had held the lamp while the doctor
probed for the bullet in Todd's side, and Grandma had directed Meg and Joyce in making swabs and bandages.

The doctor had said Todd must not be moved for several days.

Every time she had wakened during the restless night, Meg
visualized her wild cousin driving through the storm with his
terrified wife beside him. What had happened to poor Marietta?

Last night, after the shooting, she had heard mutterings
among the men. "Send the sheriff after him!" "What good
would it do? The Donahues are beyond the law—the law of
Sheriff Ramsey, at any rate." "I hear Dan Cochran's going to
run against him, come fall." "About time we had a sheriff as
can keep those wild Donahues in line."

Meg's conscience pricked and she turned restlessly on her pillow. Hadn't accepting all that she had from Uncle Barney

made her a part of his household and family? So, wasn't *she* included in that derogatory expression of contempt, the wild Donahues? What could she do? She felt pulled apart, drawn by her knowledge of right on one side and a sense of loyalty and obligation to her uncle on the other. How she needed Grandma's counsel!

Suddenly she remembered Calvin and his secret passengers. What had happened to them during the storm? They must have been out in the worst of it, just as Mike and Marietta had been. Well, Calvin was resourceful and had a clear head, not befuddled by drink as was Mike's. One could count on Calvin; he'd know what to do in an emergency. But Mike——

Grandma Lenfesty lent cotton dresses to the girls when they arose, and provided sheets in which to wrap their party dresses. In the kitchen they found her pouring gruel in a bowl for Todd. As they sat down to breakfast she took a tray upstairs to him.

Later, at the front door, Grandma assured Meg that she would take care of Todd and that Grandpa would drive him out to Sycamore Park just as soon as the doctor said he could be moved. Meg tried to thank the older woman for the party; tried to express her regret at the disgraceful behavior of her cousin. Her eyes filled with tears in her earnest desire to apologize.

Mrs. Lenfesty patted her hand understandingly. "Don't fret, dear. Remember Mike Donahue is married to my granddaughter, as well as being your cousin. Neither of us can deny the relationship. Please look after Marietta for us. We all feel so helpless where she is concerned. You are the only one who can aid her."

Outside, Grandpa drove Todd's team up to the front gate. The girls put their best dresses and hoops in the back and climbed into the front seat. Meg had never driven a team of horses, but she took the reins from Grandpa without fear. After last night, who was afraid of horses?

Grandpa reached in the pocket of his coat and drew out a newspaper which he handed to Joyce.

"Take this to your father. I think he and Calvin will be interested in a piece I marked there on the front page. I believe something important happened last week in Illinois. The Republicans nominated a man named Lincoln to run for United States senator. That piece there tells what he said in his acceptance speech. I doubt if he can beat Douglas, but he said things in that speech that needed saying."

"I'll give it to Pa," Joyce said as they drove away.

The girls forgot the newspaper as they drove through the sloppy streets of Rollins. The rain was only a mist now, but the puddles of water and deep muddy ruts bore witness to last night's deluge. Meg wondered if there really was something to the Donahues' having a way with horses. She liked the feel of the reins in her hands and the thought that it was Meg Donahue who decided which way the horses would take the carriage.

"Do you think I would dare come in to see if Marietta is all right?" Joyce asked as they reached the Pike.

"Certainly. After all, Sycamore Park is my home, you are my friend, and I am a Donahue." Meg slapped the reins on the horses' backs as she had seen Todd do. "You come in for a while, then I'll drive you on to your house."

The big clock upstairs was striking eleven as Meg and Joyce climbed the staircase. Meg dropped her sheet-wrapped dress on the bed in her room and led Joyce through the hall to Marietta's and Mike's room. Meg was about to knock on the closed door when it was opened by Millie. Seeing them, Millie put her finger to her lips and closed the door behind her.

"She just fell asleep. I've been sitting with her for the last hour." Millie led them away from the door. "Maybe you girls can tell me what happened last night. That poor child would only shake her head and moan when I asked her. She is so stopped up with a cold she can scarcely breathe or talk. Said she got wet last night."

The girls related Mike's fiendish escapade. Millie shook her head and clicked her tongue.

"One of these days that man is going to come up against somebody as isn't afraid of him, a person as cruel as he is. You mark my word, Mike Donahue will come to a bad end. The idea! Shooting his own brother, and the only one of the lot that's decent too." Millie looked at Joyce. "What your poor sister has suffered at the hands of that man. She'll be lucky if she don't get a bad spell of sickness from being out with that devil in last night's storm. There was such a chill wind blowing, and her drenched to the skin too."

Tilda gave them some food in the kitchen. Adelaide came in before they were finished to ask about Todd and how the shooting had occurred. Meg again described the sordid episode.

Adelaide bit her lip and turned away. "Mike and his drunken didoes again," she muttered. "I guess the Lord knew what He was doing to take Ma when He did. She's been spared this."

Meg pitied Adelaide.

It was early afternoon by the time Meg got Joyce home and started back to Sycamore Park. The sun shone and the air was clear and comfortably cool. What a delightful change from yesterday, Meg thought, letting the horses mosey along slowly. She held the reins in one hand, the other dropped down on the seat. Imagine, she thought, Meg Donahue driving a team of horses with one hand! If only she could do as well with her confused thinking about her relatives as she was with her horsemanship! Her hand touched something sticking up at the back of the seat cushion.

For goodness sake! It was the newspaper Joyce's grandfather had given her. Well, it would give her an excuse to ride over tomorrow to take it to the Lenfestys, and maybe Calvin would be there then.

A few miles farther on she saw a surrey approaching. She stopped. It looked like—— It was Calvin! He recognized her at the same time, pulled his horses into a lane, hopped out, and climbed in beside her.

His suit was wrinkled and he hadn't shaved, but he looked fine to Meg even so.

"I'm just getting home," he said, "and look a sight," he added apologetically. "Had to wait till they dried my clothes at Ike's place before I could start back. What are you doing way over here? And look at you, driving a team too!"

"Do you have time to hear what happened at my party after you left?"

Calvin nodded and Meg told her story for the third time.

"Why that dirty ornery skunk!" Calvin exclaimed. "Shooting his own brother and dragging Sis around like a dishrag. I'd like to get my hands on him!" He clenched his fists.

"Don't ever tangle with Mike," Meg pleaded. "He shot his own brother; he might kill you."

"He should be put in jail. Just wait till we get a new sheriff and he will be," Calvin predicted. "Sheriff Ramsey should be chasing Donahues instead of runaway slaves." He scowled.

Meg picked up the newspaper in her lap. "This morning your grandfather gave Joyce this. He said he had marked a piece on the front page for you and your father to read. Something about politics, I guess."

Calvin unfolded the paper and read the marked portion. A long "Hmmm" came from his lips. "That's plain enough for anybody, I'd say." He looked at Meg. "It's part of the acceptance speech of the Republican nominee for senator of Illinois, a man named Lincoln."

"I don't know much about politics," Meg confessed.

"Well, you could learn. I think women should know what's going on even if they can't vote," Calvin stated.

Meg observed his face, browned by days in the fields under the hot Indiana sun. Even though it bristled with whiskers, she thought it a handsome face. Last night she had felt the hard callus of his hand as she held onto it when he swung her on the corners in the reel. What a strong man he was!

"Why don't you read it to me," she said. Calvin was smart; she had better try to understand what this was all about.

"All right." Calvin put a foot on the dashboard and leaned back. "I'll just read what Lincoln said in his acceptance speech. It's all about the slavery question, of course." Calvin began to read aloud.

"'If we could first know where we are, and whither we are tending, we could better judge what to do, and how to do it. We are now far into the fifth year since a policy was initiated with the avowed object . . . of putting an end to slavery agitation. . . . In my opinion, it will not cease until a crisis shall have been reached and passed. "A house divided against itself cannot stand." I believe this government cannot endure permanently half slave and half free. I do not expect the Union to be dissolved—I do not expect the house to fall—but I do expect it will cease to be divided. It will become all one thing, or all the other.'"

Calvin paused. "I like the way he says things, plain and uncomplicated."

"Yes," Meg returned. "Even I understood what he was talking about. His words are as clear as Donati's comet in a starry sky," she added, thinking how beautifully Calvin read.

Calvin smiled at her appreciatively. "You hit the nail right on the head, Meg. Clear as the comet, but kind of frightening and terrible too; like the comet's fiery tail. Wish we had a Lincoln in Indiana," he added seriously.

Meg smiled at his fervor. "Why not wish for a Lincoln in every state," she remarked facetiously.

"In the right place, I imagine we'd need only one," Calvin said thoughtfully.

Meg was up early, Monday, July 5. On this racing day she was going to be able to watch the races at close range. Yesterday, from the front porch, she had watched the men arrange benches in a shaded section reserved for the ladies who were expected. And the governor himself was to attend. He had made a speech in Rollins the day before and was planning to watch the races at Sycamore Park today. Meg had never seen a governor and the thought of one near at hand excited her.

Marietta had been out of bed three days, but she still had a cold and coughed frequently. In fact, Mike said she coughed so much at night he couldn't sleep, so he had moved to the jockey house. Meg thought it good riddance. Since his wild behavior on her birthday, Meg couldn't bear the sight of him. Todd had been brought home the Thursday before and life was going on at Sycamore Park almost as though the shooting had never occurred.

As Meg brushed her hair before the mirror, she wondered if her cousins had run the visitors horses tired last night. Probably, even though she had not wakened to observe what was going on at the race track.

By ten o'clock the Pike was cloudy with dust raised by the vehicles on their way to Sycamore Park. The grove beyond the stables was filled with picnickers.

At twelve o'clock Meg stood on the porch with Marietta and Adelaide and watched the governor and his party arrive.

"My, doesn't he look grand in his tall silk hat!" Meg said as the Governor left his carriage and was escorted to a place of honor near the area reserved for the ladies. "And who is the lady with the beautiful sunshade?"

"His wife," Adelaide told her. "With the governor and his lady here, who knows? The Sycamore Park race track might become respectable."

"Mike says the governor has entered a horse," Marietta said slowly.

"Well, knowing Pa," Adelaide said grimly, "I'd say that chances are the governor's horse will be allowed to win at least one race. Pa knows which side his bread is buttered on."

Meg saw Marietta shake her head despairingly, but she made no reply to Adelaide's comment.

Wearing her white lawn figured with pink rosebuds, and carrying a pink ruffled parasol provided by Adelaide, Meg made her way down the hill toward the track. Marietta hadn't felt well enough to accompany her, and Adelaide said she had seen too many races in her life already.

Crowds of men had gathered all along the track. Some were dressed in fine broadcloth, others in homespun; some smoked cigars, some corncob pipes, and others chewed tobacco.

Meg tried to close her ears to the curses and oaths she heard on all sides and hurried across the track to the ladies' benches. She found a place on a bench shaded by a maple. She put down her parasol and began fanning with her birthday fan.

There was a buzz of conversation among the ladies, and Meg could feel the excitement in the high pitch of their voices. Probably being at such a wicked place as Sycamore Park excited them, Meg thought grimly. It was a good thing they did not know she was a Donahue or they would not want her to sit near them.

She looked up the hill at the brick house on top. How picturesque it was from here. One would never think from its appearance that it sheltered so much meanness. Meg sniffed the air. That must be the odor of meat roasting over the barbecue pits, she thought. She wondered if the Indians she had seen arriving since early morning were consuming Uncle Barney's whisky as well as the free food he provided. And would the sounds of their drunkenness reach the ladies here?

"Well, look who is coming this way, bold as brass," Meg heard a woman on the next bench say. "It's that low-down Mike Donahue. That's his wife with him. She was Marietta Lenfesty you know, from one of the best families in the county. What she ever saw in him, I'll never know."

Meg watched Mike swagger across the track with Marietta, beautifully dressed, on his arm. Meg surmised that Mike had forced his wife to dress in her finery and come to the race track in spite of her indisposition. Just look at him! He was taking her right over to the governor!

"Well, of all the gall!" the lady in the rear said in a loud voice. "I do believe he's going to sit by the governor. No, I guess he's leaving. He just introduced his wife. Well, from all I hear she's an angel, good enough to sit with the highest in the land."

Meg saw the governor's wife engage Marietta in conversation as Mike proceeded to the stables.

Meg stayed at the races all afternoon. During a race she would rise and stand with the other ladies nearer the track as the horses came thundering by. What beauty and grace there was in running horses, their nostrils spread wide, necks outstretched, tails flying, and their thin legs carrying them over the track at unbelievable speeds. That was the only fault she had to find with horse racing, it was over too quickly. She wondered how fast Blackie could run. Sometime when no one was around she would like to try him out on the track. She grinned to herself. She was thinking like a horsy Donahue for sure.

The last race was at five, and shortly thereafter the crowd

of spectators began to disperse. Meg saw the governor's carriage drive up for him and his wife; he took off his tall hat and bowed to Marietta; his wife took Marietta's hand. After the governor had spent an afternoon with her cousin's wife, Meg was sure he must think Mike Donahue a respectable man.

She joined Marietta as the governor's carriage drove away.

"I thought you didn't feel well enough to come," she said as they crossed the track and walked up the hill toward the house.

Marietta blew her nose. "Mike wanted me to be with the governor and his wife. They are very nice people."

"Your cold seems worse," Meg observed.

"I expect it was the dust." Marietta wiped her eyes. "I'll be all right."

The two were surprised to find Jethro Ogleby waiting for them at the front steps when they reached the house.

"Mrs. Donahue, could I speak to you for a minute?" He glanced uncertainly at Meg. Meg took the hint and climbed the steps. She could hear only faint murmurs of conversation as she reached the door.

She had just put Adelaide's parasol on a table in the hall, when Marietta entered, her face troubled. She looked around, saw that they were alone, then whispered to Meg:

"Meg, Jethro found two runaways in the haymow of the cow barn, just now. He says he slipped them into the house through the side door and hid them in the closet under the stairs. The sheriff and all his deputies are at the track. You and I must try to get them away tonight. They won't be safe in that closet. Adelaide or one of the boys might look in there. Your room is the only safe place until dark."

Assuring themselves that the front of the house was deserted, they opened the closet door and drew out a frightened woman with a little boy in her arms. The couple quickly followed Meg up to her room, Marietta back of them. Inside, with the door closed, they were safe for the moment.

"Now what can we do for you?" Marietta asked kindly. "I expect you're hungry."

"Yes ma'm, and we're dirty and tired. If I could wash my boy, please."

Meg poured water from her pitcher into the washbasin, took soap from the drawer, and unfolded a towel.

While the woman lathered the four-year-old boy's face, Marietta laid her plan before Meg.

"Jethro is saddling my horse. I'll ride over home and tell Calvin. You get some food for them. I think the kitchen is empty; Tilda and Lizzie went to see Mrs. Eakins and Millie is in town. They won't be back until around eight. Adelaide and Todd are the only ones in the house. You let them rest in here until dark. Do you think you could take them the back way, by the orchards to River Road, after dark; the way you went to Mrs. Guthro's, remember?"

Meg's throat tightened with excitement. "I think so."

"All right. I'll change my dress. I'll tell Calvin to wait for you on River Road."

Meg went down to the deserted kitchen, took a tray from the cupboard, and then proceeded to cover it with food from the well-stocked pantry. She put a clean towel over it and started for the stairs. She was just putting her foot on the first step when Adelaide came out of the sitting room. She glanced at the tray in Meg's hands.

"Oh, I see you fixed a supper tray for Todd. I was going to do that," she said.

"It's not for Todd," she admitted. "I—I am a little tired tonight and thought I would eat in my room and go to bed early," she finished lamely, hoping God would forgive her for such a lie.

Adelaide looked at her closely. "You don't appear tired, I must say. In fact, you seem very alert to me, cheeks pink and a sparkle in your eyes; excited I'd say. I guess the races must have sent you into a tizzy. All right, run along. I'll fix Todd's tray pretty soon."

Meg sighed with relief as Adelaide returned to the sitting room. What if her cousin had lifted the towel and seen the quantity of food? she wondered as she climbed to her room.

Meg watched the woman and child eat hungrily from the tray. Her name was Callie, the woman said, and her boy was Bertie. When they had finished eating, Meg tried to persuade them to lie on her bed to rest, but Callie declined, saying it wouldn't be right, that the floor here was better than any place they had slept during the past two weeks. Unable to induce Callie to use the bed, Meg spread a comforter on the floor and placed pillows there for the two weary heads.

She did not dare leave the room for fear of running into Adelaide again. She sat in her rocking chair as dusk descended and watched the sleeping forms on the floor by the window.

Now that the more respectable element had departed from the track, the hangers-on became rowdy and noisy. Meg saw lanterns appear around the stables and in the trees as it became dark. She knew that this roistering would go on all night if it followed the pattern of the other racing day, and that Uncle Barney and her cousins would not be returning to the house.

She removed her rosebud dress and put on a black one. She wanted to be as inconspicuous as possible in the flight to River Road. The clock in the hall struck half-past eight. She sat down to wait until nine, the time Marietta had named for her to leave with her two charges.

The noise down the hill had become so loud now that Meg could not even hear the squeak of her own rocking chair as she waited for the clock to strike again.

XIII

A NIGHT TO REMEMBER

Meg touched Callie's shoulder as the clock finished striking nine. The woman was awake at once and on her feet, her sleeping child in her arms. Meg tiptoed into the dark hall to reconnoiter. She had been sitting in the dark so long her eyes were accustomed to it. Todd's door and Adelaide's were closed. What had Marietta told Adelaide about riding to her family's, and would Marietta spend the night there? Well, she mustn't worry about that, she had enough on her mind just to accomplish her own mission.

She looked over the banister to the hall below. All was quiet and dark. Returning to her room, she signaled Callie, and the woman followed her silently. At the foot of the stairs Meg paused, her hand on the saddle at the newel post.

Little Bertie shifted his head on his mother's shoulder while she patted his back comfortingly.

Meg took them out the side door. There were bolts on all the doors but they were seldom fastened, as there was sure to be one Donahue out at all hours of any night. Meg was confident that she would be able to get back in when she returned.

She led Callie to the back of the house, around the smokehouse, chicken coop, and cow barn. It was a good thing, she thought, that all the dogs were at the stables, adding their barks and howls to the general din coming from that direction.

When they reached the orchards, Meg said, "Callie, let me carry Bertie. You must be tired."

"Oh, no ma'm. My arms is just used to him. When you loves a chile, his heft is no burden at all. That's why I run away, to keep him with me."

By the time they reached the cornfields, the noise at the race track could barely be heard. Meg, for the most part, kept her eyes on the ground, trying to keep to the path. Now and again she glanced up at the comet trailing across the sky and thought of Calvin. Would he be at the appointed place to carry this weary mother and her child to safety?

Calvin *was* waiting at the fence on River Road. "Are you all right, Meg," he said softly as he took Bertie from Callie's arms.

"Yes. Did Marietta ride back to Sycamore Park?"

"No. Ma wouldn't let her. That girl is sick, Meg. Ma put her to bed. You tell Mike in the morning."

Meg watched Callie climb the fence and take her son from Calvin. He pointed to the wagon on the road; Callie obediently walked to it and crawled in.

At the fence Calvin looked down at Meg on the other side. "Think you can get back all right?" he asked concernedly.

"Of course. Don't worry about me. Just get Callie and her boy to safety," Meg said. She waited until the wagon disappeared into the darkness.

Meg had never been so far from home at night by herself. The sky, a vast star-studded dome above, with its brilliant comet, was friendly enough, but the cornfield seemed full of lurking danger. The rustle of cornstalks in the breeze whispered of unseen assailants, planning to pounce on Meg as she hurried along.

Near the apple orchard she paused. What was that which loomed ahead in the path? It moved slightly, then swayed. Oh dear, it might be a drunken rowdy who had wandered here from the track!

Meg lifted her skirts, left the path, and ran pell-mell through the apple orchard, through the peach orchard, and to the other path beyond. How fortunate, she thought, that she knew about this alternate way to get back to the house, along the creek.

With the two orchards between her and the unknown shadow, she stopped running and walked to catch her breath. Now, at this distance, she wondered if it had really been a man she had seen. It was so easy to see danger in a shadow at night when one was alone.

The cabin on the creek came into view and Meg stopped short! There was a faint light shining through the covered window on this side! What should she do? To get to the field back of the big house, she had to pass near the cabin. She left the path and huddled under a peach tree. Should she go back to the other path?

Suddenly she grew tense, the light inside was extinguished; she heard voices and the rattle of the lock on the front door. Two men came around to the side nearest the peach orchard and stood talking, within twenty feet of Meg, hidden in the shadows.

"You can pass it anywhere." It was Mike's voice. "Ross and I have fooled everybody around here with it. You are getting a bargain at forty cents on the dollar. I don't see what you're complaining about."

"I know, Mike, but I'm not in good with the law in my county like you Donahues. Like as not I'll get caught first crack out of the box," the other man replied.

"Oh, quit your bellyaching. You've got by with horse-thieving all these years. I know good and well you stole that horse you raced today. So why get so squeamish about passing Donahue-made money. I warrant in a month you'll be back for more."

Meg gulped and leaned against the tree. So, counterfeiting had been added to the long list of Donahue crimes! Surely a day of retribution would come to this family of hers. The law had to catch up with them. When it did, would she be held accountable too for all their dishonesty? Wasn't she accepting her keep from them?

When the two disappeared in the direction of the stables, Meg continued along the creek, went through the field, climbed the fence, and made her way wearily around the house to the side door. The racket from the stables was audible again. How good it would be to go to bed. She was sure even the noise would not keep her from sleeping. It must be almost eleven o'clock she judged, and it seemed she had been on this mission all night.

She turned the doorknob and pushed on the door. Nothing happened! She put her knee against it and shoved. It wouldn't budge! Who could have bolted this door and why?

She went around and tried the front door; it was fastened tight. She dropped into a chair on the porch. How tired she was! The fires in the barbecue pits below were blazing high. Were they getting ready to roast more meat over hot coals again? Probably. Millie had said they would be eating and drinking all night down there.

Was she going to have to spend the night here on the front porch? She would try the kitchen door, but she hadn't much hope. Whoever had locked up would not have missed that one either. And he hadn't, nor even the big flat cellar door that sloped down from the house.

It wouldn't do to waken Adelaide or Todd, and Tilda, Lizzie, and Millie slept on the third floor; she wouldn't be able to make them hear. There was nothing else for it; Meg Donahue must spend the night outdoors! She could go to the cow barn she supposed, but since it was warm, she decided that she preferred the back porch.

She laid down in a corner and tried pillowing her head on her arm. How hard the boards were! Now she appreciated what Callie and other runaways went through to gain freedom, with never a real bed on which to rest their weary bodies. She thought of the bed she had made on the floor for Callie and her son. Oh, if she only had that soft comforter and pillow out here!

A good thing she had on this old black dress. She smoothed down her skirt and felt the bulk of her petticoats beneath. Petticoats!

She got up, raised the dress, and removed two of her four petticoats. Folding them, she stretched herself out again and put the bulky bundle of petticoats under her head for a pillow. That was better!

She could see the stars from here and Donati's comet. Was Calvin watching it too, as he drove his human cargo along River Road? And was he thinking of her, as she was of him? What a night this was turning out to be! Certainly a night to remember!

Dogs howled at the stables in accompaniment to some raucous singing. But Meg heard neither. She slept soundly on the back porch.

She wakened at half-past five when Millie opened the door. Millie gasped as she saw Meg sit up and rub her shoulders.

"Why, Meg Donahue, whatever are you doing out here, this time of morning?"

Meg stood up and smiled at the woman's astonishment. "It was so noisy last night, I couldn't sleep, so I came outside to—to look at the stars and—and the comet," she said. Oh, the lies she was telling! But it couldn't be helped. "And when I tried to get back in, the house was locked tighter than a new boot. So—I had to sleep out here." Meg picked up her makeshift pillow.

"I'll never complain again about wearing lots of petticoats. They make a very satisfactory pillow."

"Why you poor child. And it's all my fault. Last night I thought I heard someone fooling around down here in the back. Couple of years ago one of those fool drunks got in the house. So, knowing none of our menfolks would be coming in till today, I just waltzed myself downstairs and locked up everything." Millie clicked her tongue. "My, my, I hope you don't catch your death, sleeping out here in the night air."

"Oh, I'm all right. But from now on I'll appreciate my bed more than I ever did before." Meg pushed back her hair. "I must get upstairs though and change my dress. I probably look awful."

Jethro approached, a full milk pail in each hand. "Miss Meg, I'm some worried. Mrs. Marietta rode off last evening after the races and her horse is not in the stable this morning. You know anything about it?" He set the pails on the porch.

Meg hesitated. She couldn't tell them what Calvin had told her, for how could she explain seeing him? "She—she said she might spend the night with her folks."

Jethro shook his head. "Well, let's hope she gets back before Mike comes up to the house. I guess this is the first time she's ever been away from here overnight, ain't it, Millie?"

"That's right. I hope her ma is doing something for that cold of hers. It worries me the way it's hung on. She ought to see a doctor."

Before combing her hair and changing her dress, Meg removed all signs of the bed on the floor in her room. She glanced out the window and shook her head in distaste at the sight. The slope down to the track was dotted with men sleeping off the effects of the night's excesses. How long would the decent people around here put up with it all? she wondered. And, sooner or later, someone would get on to what was going on in the cabin on the creek. Sycamore Park was so beautiful on the surface, but oh, how rotten at the core.

If only she could do something to change things, but so far all she had done was to accept Uncle Barney's generosity—a home, fine clothes, and a beautiful horse, all paid for with ill-gotten money, perhaps even counterfeit. But hadn't she come on the scene too late to change the Donahues? If only Todd could be saved from following in his brothers' footsteps.

Mike came to the house at noon and raised a disturbance at not finding his wife there, and even more when he discovered that she had been gone all night. He saddled a horse and rode off toward the Lenfestys'. Meg wished she could have stopped him.

When he returned, Marietta rode beside him, looking as though she scarcely had the strength to cling to her saddle. Millie and Meg helped her upstairs, while Mike stood below shouting what he would do if she ever left home again.

They put her to bed. In the hall Millie clenched her fists and said, "There just ought to be a law to protect women from husbands like him. That poor lamb can't stand much more."

Late in the afternoon Todd left his room and sat on the front porch with Meg.

"Guess I lost a lot of blood," he remarked when Meg mentioned that he was pale. "How did you like the races yesterday?" he asked, changing the subject.

"They were very exciting, and such a big crowd of people too. A shame you couldn't be up to see it all." Meg wondered why he ignored the shooting.

"Fourth of July races are nothing new to me. I spent the day in the South." Todd put his feet up in another chair, leaned back and closed his eyes.

"I don't understand."

"For the past week, while I was in bed, I took your advice and read Addie's copy of *Uncle Tom's Cabin*. Finished it yesterday."

"Well?"

"It's a fine book. Makes a fellow feel he's right there. That slavery business is quite a problem. Yes sir, quite a problem. I had no idea, no idea at all, that there was so much misery because of it."

"Calvin says we have to do something about it," Meg said. "And that all we need is a leader for the cause, since Mrs. Stowe's book has paved the way."

"Calvin's right, I expect. He was always a real smart boy in school," Todd said.

On impulse Meg asked, "Todd, aren't you going to do anything about Mike shooting you?"

Todd shifted his feet. "Oh, I doubt it. He didn't know what he was doing. Under the influence, you know."

Meg nodded. "He certainly was drunk, if that's what you mean. But Todd, what I'd like to know is why Marietta married him. Do you know?"

Todd sat up, took his feet from the chair, and stared closely at his cousin's face. "I don't know exactly." He paused. "Pa sent me to town on an errand that night, the night they eloped. I think the other boys know the particulars, but they never talked about them to me. I guess I was as surprised as most folks when I heard they were married. But Meg, you mustn't fret yourself about it. They're married and that's that."

"Yes, I suppose so. But Mike is so—so——"

"Yes, Meg. I expect I know Mike better than you do. You can't tell me a thing but what I know more, a lot more. Seems like the devil himself has taken him over, body and soul. Poor Ma, how she used to cry over his badness. I recollect that once some gypsies camped on our land down by the river. I was a little fellow riding there with Mike. Mike got off his horse and lit into some of them with a whip and ordered them off, swearing and cussing like sixty. They packed up in a hurry and were on their way. But an old gypsy woman stood looking at Mike before she got in her wagon, shook her fist, and said some strange-sounding words. One of the men shouted at her and said, 'Come on, Grandma, he'll come to a bad end even without your curse.'" Todd paused. "That's always worried me. A gypsy curse is not a trifle, you know."

Thinking of this conversation later, Meg decided that whatever the gypsy had in mind for Mike, he deserved, and then some.

Marietta was still confined to bed on Sunday, and Meg drove to church alone. Outside the church after the service, the Lenfestys gathered about Meg, inquiring after Marietta's health. Meg was so sorry for Mrs. Lenfesty, her motherly concern for her eldest so apparent in her face.

Meg did what she could to reassure her. Millie and Tilda were taking good care of Marietta, she said, and Meg was sure Marietta would be up and around in no time.

"Meg, come home to dinner with us," Mrs. Lenfesty urged.

"Please do," Joyce enjoined. "Grandma and Grandpa Lenfesty are coming out from town. They'll probably be there when we get home."

Meg glanced at Calvin, standing by his father. He smiled and nodded.

"All right, I will," she agreed. Joyce got into the Donahue buggy with Meg, saying she would keep her company. Calvin looked up at the girls as Meg picked up the reins.

"You can ride with her this time, dear Sister," he said with a grin, "but you wouldn't be there if I hadn't come to church horseback."

"Brother dear, you could tie your horse behind her buggy and ride inside beside her," Joyce teased.

"So I could."

"Oh, come on, Meg," Joyce urged. "Let's go before he makes me get down."

Meg laughed happily as she drove away, enjoying this vying for a place beside her.

At the Lenfestys' Nancy and Peter claimed it was their turn to sit beside Meg at the table, as Betsy and Sarah had done so the last time she had taken dinner with them.

Meg had not seen the elder Lenfestys since the morning after her disastrous birthday party in June. Grandma's eyes misted as she asked Meg about Marietta.

Meg was impressed again by the warmth and gentility of this family. They ate slowly, conversing intelligently all the while. The children were quiet, behaving according to the admonition Meg's grandmother had so often quoted to her, that children should be seen but not heard.

She listened to Grandma Lenfesty tell Calvin's mother of the tea she had given the week before for a missionary and his wife, just back from China. She listened to the talk of politics between Grandpa Lenfesty, Calvin's father, and Calvin. Calvin was able to hold his own with the two older men.

"Thousands of men are out of work in Chicago," Grandpa was saying.

Calvin's father helped himself to a slice of bread and proceeded to butter it slowly. "I heard about that. Father, did you read what some fellow said in Congress? That whatever was said against slavery, at least there was no unemployment and no hunger among the Negro field hands of the South."

Calvin broke in. "But there are some things worse than unemployment and hunger."

Grandpa pursed his lips and nodded. "Man does not live by bread alone, that's true. As that man Lincoln said, 'If we could know where we are and whither we are tending, we could better judge what to do and how to do it.' The Democratic newspapers are calling Lincoln an agitator, a blatherskite, and a radical since he made that speech in June."

"But something's got to be done!" Calvin's eyes grew intense. "Why, do you know, I read that it's estimated that right now at least ten thousand Negroes a year are being smuggled right from the jungles of Africa and sold in this country!"

Mr. Lenfesty looked grave and said, "Calm youself, Son. Something will be done when we get the right man in the White House."

"In the meantime," Grandpa put in, "we'd better concern ourselves with politics right here in our own county. We've got to get new men in office and clean up our own affairs. Come November, after the election, this county is going to see a great exodus of all the undesirables we've had in our midst for much too long a time."

Meg looked down at her plate. Did he mean the wild Donahues?

XIV

A SHOOTING

Meg was used to hot summers in Cincinnati, but Indiana heat in July and August, she decided, was really outdoing anything she had ever known before. She got up each morning before five in order to get her part of the housework done before the sun made even breathing a chore.

Marietta was able to be out of bed by the middle of July. She said her cold was gone, but Meg noticed that she coughed frequently and, as Millie said, looked as if a puff of wind would blow her away. She did not ride horseback, nor did she visit her family or go to church, but stayed close to the big brick house in Sycamore Park. Meg wondered if Mike had issued orders that she was not to leave the premises.

Meg saw very little of Uncle Barney and his sons, save at mealtime; then they ate quickly, saying little, and left as soon as they finished. For all of their wickedness, Meg had to admit they were hard workers, and there was more than enough to keep them busy from sunup to sundown at Sycamore Park. By August, Todd was able to do his part again at the stables and in the fields.

It was strange, Meg thought, that the fact that Mike had shot his brother was ignored by the whole family. Even Todd shrugged it off as though Mike had merely shoved him in a friendly encounter. Queer people, these Donahues!

Meg became better acquainted with Lizzie Ridenour. One afternoon she walked down by the creek and found the child playing there, dabbling her feet in the water and making a small dam of sticks and stones. Meg admired the doll that lay on the bank beside Lizzie. It was a gift from Mrs. Marietta, the little girl informed her. Meg offered to make doll clothes for it.

This led to many pleasant afternoons on the front porch with the two of them cutting and sewing a new wardrobe for Lizzie's Anna Marie.

And so it was that late in August, Meg accompanied Lizzie to her grandmother's to spend the night at the tollhouse. Meg rode Blackie, with Lizzie perched behind her.

"One reason Grandma wants me to visit her is to try on some dresses she's making me—school dresses for next winter," Lizzie told Meg as they rode along.

"You are doing such nice sewing for Anna Marie, you'll be making your own clothes before long," Meg returned.

"When I grow up I want to wear dresses just like Mrs. Marietta's. I'd like to be as beautiful as she is too, but Ma says there'll never be anybody as pretty as she is. But I tell you, I'm not going to have a husband like hers. I'm scared of him and I think Mrs. Marietta is too. I'm going to get me a husband like Mr. Todd or maybe like Mrs. Marietta's brother. You know him?"

Meg smiled and gave Blackie's neck a pat. "Yes, I know Calvin."

"He's nice. He stopped and talked to me about Mrs. Marietta one day when I was at Grandma's."

Meg found the tollhouse as interesting as its keeper, Mrs. Eakins. The gate across the road, she discovered, could be raised or lowered from within the house or outside, depending upon where Mrs. Eakins was when a traveler came by.

"Do you have to get up in the night to collect the toll when someone wants by?" Meg asked.

"Of course," replied the wiry old lady. "Nobody slips through that gate day or night without paying. I sleep right here in the front room and hoofbeats a mile away wake me and I'm ready for 'em time they get here. I got me a shotgun handy too, in case anybody thinks he can outsmart me."

"I'm sure no one could outsmart you, Mrs. Eakins," Meg said admiringly.

When they sat down to supper, Mrs. Eakins said, "Now, Miss Donahue, suppose you tell me all about that ruckus at the party Old Lady Lenfesty gave for you in town. 'Course, I've heard all about it before, but I'd like to get it straight from the horse's mouth, so to speak."

Meg picked up her fork, thinking that there was little that went on in this part of Indiana that the tollgate keeper did not know. "It was an accident, I think, Mrs. Eakins. Mike's gun went off and just happened to strike Todd."

"Oh, go on with you!" Mrs. Eakins cocked her head on one side and gave a cackling laugh. "You know good and well Mike Donahue was drunk as a lord and shooting things up to a fare-you-well!"

"Mrs. Eakins, I don't approve of such behavior any more than you do, but like Marietta, there's not a thing I can do about it." Meg wished they could change the subject.

"Well, there are those who think they *can* do something about the Donahues. I hear rumors from time to time. And the latest is that even their races are not on the up-and-up, that their horses are not always the fastest, even though they usually win."

Meg lowered her eyes, feeling sure the all-knowing Mrs. Eakins would read her mind if she looked into them.

"Grandma, did you have enough left from any of my dresses to make some doll clothes?" Lizzie asked.

Meg welcomed the chance to discuss the child's growing ability with a needle.

They sat in the yard after supper while Mrs. Eakins related tales of the early days when she had come to Indiana as a bride in 1825, and had helped her husband build a cabin and clear the land. Now and again she would hop up to collect a toll and converse with the traveler.

Meg took a lighted candle and went upstairs with Lizzie about half-past eight. They slept in the front bedroom, directly over the one Mrs. Eakins occupied below. Lizzie dropped to sleep almost at once, but Meg lay beside her and thought of Mrs. Eakins' early life, filled with difficulties, encounters with Indians, and most of all with hard work and sorrow; she had buried six children in infancy. Of the seven she had borne, only Tilda lived. Mrs. Eakins was a brave, resourceful woman, Meg decided before she dropped to sleep.

Something wakened her suddenly! She looked into the dark and, for a moment, could not remember where she was. Moonlight streamed into the window near the road. It must have been the clop-clop of approaching hoofbeats that had wakened her. She supposed Mrs. Eakins was up and waiting to collect the toll. Slipping out of bed quietly, she went to the window to see the transaction.

The horseback rider, she observed, was galloping toward the gate as though he did not know that it blocked the road. Upon reaching it the horse reared on its hind legs and let out a frightened neigh. The rider swayed in the saddle, then to Meg's horror, pulled a gun from his belt and fired it into the air!

"Get out here, you old witch, and lift that gate," he shouted with an oath.

Meg shuddered. It was her cousin Mike!

Lizzie was beside her and the two watched the little drama which took place in the moonlight.

"Pay your toll and I will," Mrs. Eakins yelled from her window.

"I'll pay you nothing, old woman. I'm Mike Donahue and I ride where I please. Raise that gate!" He flourished his gun.

"You don't scare me one bit, you good-for-nothing! Why, I've known you since you was a pup. I got my shotgun aimed at you and unless you want to be filled with buckshot, drop that pistol! You hear?"

Mike hesitated, then, seeing the barrel of the shotgun extended from the open window, he dropped his firearm.

Mrs. Eakins came outside in her white, long-sleeved nightgown, her hair in a braid down her back. Shotgun still in hand, she walked calmly out into the road and extended her hand for the toll.

Muttering all the while, Mike paid it. The old woman pulled on the rope and the gate went up. She handed him his gun and he rode off in the moonlight.

Lizzie sighed as her grandmother disappeared into the house, then she giggled. "I guess my grandma's a match for anybody, isn't she? Even Mike Donahue."

"She is indeed," Meg agreed as they went back to bed.

Two days before the fall racing day, September 1, men began to arrive from as far away as Kentucky and Virginia, bringing their race horses with them. Meg went to the stables in the afternoon to get her horse and paused to watch the visitors running their entries to accustom them to the Donahue track. She admired the fractious thoroughbreds trotting around the course. It was too bad they had so little chance of winning on Wednesday, she thought.

Hurrying around the corner of Blackie's stable, she ran head

on into a strange man, brushing against his shoulder in her
haste.

"Oh, I beg your pardon," she apologized.

"That's quite all right," he said in a soft Southern drawl, lifting his hat. "I didn't expect to encounter a charming lady out
here. But I must say it is an agreeable surprise." He smiled and
his teeth showed white and even, in the midst of his short black
beard, the kind so fashionable among young men.

"I was hurrying out to saddle my horse and wasn't looking
where I was going," Meg explained.

"You live here?" the man questioned.

"Yes. I'm Meg Donahue."

"But I thought there was only one Miss Donahue."

"Oh, you mean Adelaide. I'm not a sister. I'm a cousin from
Cincinnati."

"I see. There's a Mrs. Donahue too, isn't there?"

"Yes. My cousin Mike's wife, Marietta."

The man looked away, then stepped aside for Meg to pass.
"Do you ladies ride often?" he asked.

"I ride almost every day, but Marietta hasn't been very well
this summer; she just sits on the front porch." Meg nodded toward the house at the top of the hill.

"Is that she up there now?" the stranger asked softly, his head
tilted back as he looked up at the house.

"Yes. She's there with Adelaide. Marietta is the one in the
blue dress."

"Her husband must be very concerned about her ill health,"
he said, not taking his eyes from the blue-gowned figure in the
distance.

Meg looked at him curiously. There was something in his
voice that made her wonder. "Perhaps you would like to go up
with me now and meet my cousin's wife," she said. He seemed
such a gentleman, she felt that Marietta might want to invite
him to dinner.

"Oh, no," he refused quickly. "I am just on my way to run my horse on the track in preparation for Wednesday." He tipped his hat and disappeared around the stable.

Meg walked on to Blackie's stall. There was something about that man! She would ask Todd about him. But how could she? She didn't even know his name.

The next evening Meg sat on the front porch with Uncle Barney and Adelaide. Marietta had gone to bed right after supper. The hot summer, Meg contemplated, had been hard on Marietta. She had the look of a drooping rose these days. Meg had intended telling her of the bearded gentleman who had asked about her yesterday, but there had been no opportunity.

Lizzie sat on the steps, running out on the lawn occasionally to chase and catch one of the innumerable fireflies that flashed on and off in the gathering dusk. Meg rocked slowly and listened to Uncle Barney and Adelaide speak of crops, horses, and plans to buy more land to add to Sycamore Park.

Looking down at the peaceful scene below, the grassy hill, the track, and the stables, Meg found it hard to remember that dishonesty, cruelty, lies, and trickery were at the root of it all. Sycamore Park was like a beautiful lady with a black and wicked heart, she mused. Was she herself becoming hardened to all the wrongdoing that she saw here every day? Was she getting so used to Donahue shenanigans that they didn't shock her as much as they did? Oh, she hoped not! But what could one seventeen-year-old girl do?

She wished she could talk to Calvin, but she hadn't seen him for three weeks; he was always in the fields or on a trip north when she rode to the Lenfestys'.

Uncle Barney got up, walked to the steps, and knocked the ashes from his pipe on a post. "Well, guess I'll get along and ride over to the jockey house and see how the boys are making out. Want to keep our visitors busy over there tonight," he said.

Meg's eyes narrowed. Outside entries would be run on the track tonight, she supposed, so the Donahues had to keep their owners occupied elsewhere.

Uncle Barney had just reached the bottom step when the quiet of the evening was shattered by a shot. Meg and Adelaide stood up, Lizzie paused in her chase of a firefly. Uncle Barney peered in the direction of the sound and muttered, "Now, what the devil——"

A shadowy horse and rider came out of the stable and thundered down the lane toward the Pike. Uncle Barney ran down the hill. Meg saw a small figure running toward him. They met at the track, spoke, then Uncle Barney ran on and the other one ran up the hill.

It was a breathless Joey who arrived at the house. "It's Jason; he's shot!" the boy cried, looking at Adelaide. "Mr. Barney said for you to get his bed ready."

Adelaide turned toward the door. "Meg, go to the kitchen and tell Tilda to boil water and Millie to give you clean rags. Joey, take a horse and ride to the jockey house and tell the other boys what has happened. One of them should ride to town for Dr. Dixon."

By the time Jason had been carried into his room by Todd, Jethro, and Uncle Barney, Meg had fulfilled her assignments, and a basin of hot water and a stack of clean rags were ready on a table beside the bed. She stood back as they put down her moaning cousin. Meg heard Adelaide click her tongue in dismay as she viewed Jason's bloody chest.

"You ride all night, if you have to," Uncle Barney was saying to Todd, "but you get him! You hear?"

"But Pa, I told you, the Kentuckian shot in self-defense. It was that black-bearded fellow who arrived yesterday, the one named Jay Parridon. He had just told Jason he intended to sleep in the stall with his horse tonight. Jason told him nobody was allowed to stay in the stables at night. Parridon insisted, so Jason started to draw on him, but the Kentuckian was quicker. The sheriff wouldn't hold him if we caught him."

"Sheriff Ramsey will hold him if I say so," Uncle Barney said grimly, looking down at his bloody son. "But you needn't wait for that; you just shoot him on sight."

"No, Pa. I won't. Instead, I'll ride in for the doctor." Todd turned away.

Uncle Barney watched helplessly as Adelaide washed away the blood. "I'll sick Mike on him," he muttered. "Mike won't shilly-shally with words about self-defense."

Meg made a hasty exit. She felt giddy in the hot upstairs room. It wouldn't help matters for her to faint there. In her own room, she held a wet cloth to her temples.

So, it had been that nice, soft-spoken man she had run into yesterday who had shot her cousin. Todd had said his name was Jay Parridon. He must have suspected something wrong about the races if he had insisted on staying with his horse. She hoped the Donahues wouldn't catch him.

Riders galloped up below; she heard the stamp of heavy boots on the stairs, then loud voices in Jason's room. The boots clomped down the stairs and the riders rode away. The Donahues were off to hunt down the Kentuckian.

Pale and shaken, Marietta appeared, candle in hand, in Meg's doorway. "Jason just died," she said. "God pity that man if they find him."

There was no racing at Sycamore Park the next day. Instead, the Donahue brothers carried Jason to the family burying ground near the river and put him beside their mother. Then they rode off again, determined to overtake Jay Parridon in his flight to Kentucky.

XV

THE TALL SUCKER
AND THE LITTLE GIANT

The Donahue boys were gone more than a week, hunting their brother's killer. Todd and Uncle Barney did not go on the search, but worked thirteen and fourteen hours every day to try to cover all the daily tasks at Sycamore Park in the absence of the avengers.

"We didn't find him, Pa," Mike told his father sullenly, as the four brothers came up to the front porch the evening of September 10. "We followed his trail all the way into Kentucky and lost it just yon side of Cornell's place. You remember, he was that fellow that stayed overnight with us last April, the one up here hunting his runaways."

Meg felt relieved that the man with the black beard had escaped Donahue reprisal.

Ben and Ross sprawled their huge frames onto the steps, while Chris threw himself down on the grass, with his arms under his head, and stared up at the evening sky. Mike sat at Marietta's feet.

Uncle Barney puffed on his pipe. "Too bad you didn't catch the varmint. Well, one thing, he'll never dare show his face at our track again. You know, now that I think on it, he was uncommonly well acquainted with our place for a fellow who had never been here, and he seemed kinda familiar. Are you sure he hadn't raced here before?"

Chris sat up. "No, Jay Parridon never was here before, Pa. I never set eyes on him till he showed up August 13. Wish now I'd run him off the place right then."

"I tried to call on your old beau, Marietta," Mike said in a deriding tone. "The Parrish place is down in that neck of the woods, you know. But pretty-boy John was not at home. His pa said he'd gone off to a race somewhere." Mike laughed unpleasantly. "I wanted to tell him how happy you are with me and that you are the best-dressed woman in Indiana."

It wasn't until Meg was in bed that a surprising idea occurred to her. The black-bearded man might have been John Parrish himself! Mrs. Guthro had described him as a handsome, smooth-shaven man; but with a black beard concealing his features——? She remembered his questions about Marietta. And the name Jay Parridon might have been his way of disguising his real one, John Parrish. Well, she'd probably never know; for one thing was certain, the man would never dare show up at Sycamore Park again.

The next day was Saturday and for all the warm sunshine on the front porch there was a feel of fall in the air. After she had shaken out her dustcloth, Meg stood at the top of the steps and noted that the leaves were falling off the poplar beyond the driveway. What would Sycamore Park be like in winter? she wondered. She wasn't sure it would be very pleasant to be snowed in here with the wild Donahues. It would be like being shut in a cage with lions and tigers. What did her cousins do when there was no racing or field work?

Adelaide came out and stood beside her. "Monday we'll start the fall cleaning," she said, her hands on her hips. "I usually start right after the fall racing day, but what with Jason's killing and the boys off after his killer, somehow I didn't have any heart for it."

"What about the races?" Meg asked. "Will they set another day?"

"I reckon. Pa's not one to pass up the chance of running his nags and making some money, even if all of his offspring were to get themselves killed. But there will have to be time for him to spread the word about the date. I allow he'll set a date in the early part of October. So in the meantime we can give the house its cleaning and get ready for winter. It's a good thing you are here to help and are a thorough worker, for Marietta won't be able to do anything with the cleaning." Adelaide frowned. "I'm worried about Marietta. She isn't a bit well; no more energy than a droopy chicken. She is in bed this morning and coughing her head off. I gave her some camomile tea and wanted to send for the doctor, but she wouldn't hear of it."

"Is there anything I can do for her?" Meg asked.

"Yes, there is. I want you to go to the Lenfestys this morning and tell her mother that she's sick and that I'd take it kindly if she'd come over and have a look at her. I don't want that girl's health on my conscience. Lord knows I've got enough on it as is." Adelaide sighed. "So you saddle up and get along."

"All right, Adelaide."

At the tollgate Mrs. Eakins took Meg's toll and asked, "Them cousins of yours catch that fellow as killed Jason?"

"No. They just got back last night, But they didn't find him."

"Too bad he didn't shoot Mike too," she muttered. "Where you off to this morning?"

"Going to the Lenfestys'. Adelaide wants Mrs. Lenfesty to come over and have a look at Marietta. She's sick."

"Yes, I heard Marietta didn't have the strength of a katydid these days. She must be in bad shape or Addie Donahue wouldn't be asking a Lenfesty to Sycamore Park. You mark my word, that devil Mike will kill that girl one of these days; kill her in one way or another!"

At the Lenfestys', Meg delivered Adelaide's message to Marietta's mother.

"I'll be there this afternoon," the lady replied, her face filled with concern for her daughter. "Oh, Meg, why oh why did she marry that man? I've asked myself that a million times. I know he's your cousin, but you know the kind of man he is."

"I do, indeed!" Meg replied, thinking that Mrs. Lenfesty didn't know the half of it.

During a brief talk with Joyce, Meg learned that Calvin was in the orchard picking apples. By the time she got back to the tollgate she wished she had ridden by the orchard to see him. But that would have been a bit bold, she supposed.

After dinner she sat on the front porch with Lizzie and listened to the child read from her school reader. When the Lenfesty buggy drove up to the steps, the little girl ran off, around the house. Meg watched Calvin get out and help his mother descend. Adelaide appeared and escorted Mrs. Lenfesty inside. Calvin took a chair beside Meg to wait for his mother.

He looked down the long vista to the race track. "Say, this is quite a sight from here. I had no idea."

"Pretty, isn't it?" Meg commented.

"Impressive, I'd say," Calvin returned. "What do you think is wrong with Sis?"

"She just can't seem to shake off the effects of that cold she caught in June," Meg replied. How brown Calvin's face was, she thought, almost as dark as the bronze andirons in the parlor. "But it seems to me that she isn't interested in getting better. She is so listless; really not the same person she was when I came."

"It's probably that devil of a husband of hers," Calvin growled.

"Shouldn't wonder."

There was silence. Meg watched a chicken hawk circle in the sky and wondered what Calvin was thinking.

"Meg," he said at last, "I've missed not seeing you for so long. Pa and I haven't been able to get to church lately, the crops have come along so fast. But I've thought about you. Thought about you a lot," he added, leaning on the chair arm nearest hers.

"That's nice, Calvin," Meg said, thinking what an inane reply to a remark that had set her heart pounding as hard as the beat of a race horse's hoofs.

"You know, Grandpa wants me to move to town this winter and work for him; learn the hardware business."

"And are you going to?" Meg remembered that it was farther to Rollins than it was to the Lenfesty farm by several miles.

"Can't make up my mind. Which would you rather have me be, a farmer or a city man?"

Meg laughed. "What I think couldn't make much difference one way or the other."

"Oh, but it does. Both Pa and Grandpa have been at me to make up my mind, each one giving me a slew of arguments until I don't know whether I'm coming or going. Now give me your opinion."

Meg looked into his clear, honest eyes. "Somehow," she said slowly, "I can't see you indoors all day weighing out nails and counting bolts. Wouldn't you miss the sky and open spaces and the challenge of working the soil, coaxing it to grow the grain?"

Calvin smiled. "You know, that's just what I've been telling myself. And now that I know we are in agreement, I'll tell Grandpa he'll have to look for another man. I thought maybe, being from a big place like Cincinnati, you preferred living in town." He looked down at the stables.

"No. I like it here in the country." Meg wondered what all this was leading up to.

"Guess most anybody'd like living at a fine place like Sycamore Park, even in the same house with Mike Donahue," he said slowly, a frown on his face.

"I would like it better," Meg returned, "if the house and grounds weren't so fine and there was more love and understanding in the family."

Calvin brightened and looked at her. "You know what, Meg Donahue, you're all right! And I've just noticed something. You're not the girl you were when you first came, but a real grown-up woman, and—if I may say so—pretty as a picture!"

"Cal Lenfesty, you are an old palaverer! Grandma always said too many compliments spoiled a girl." Meg laughed gaily and wished she could sit here forever listening to him.

At that moment Mrs. Lenfesty and Adelaide came out the door.

Monday, Uncle Barney and his sons moved to the jockey house to get out of the way of Adelaide's cleaning storm. The spring ritual was repeated and the house was in turmoil for two weeks. This time, before carpets were tacked down, a thick layer of fresh straw was strewn over the floors, to keep winter's cold from finding its way up through the cracks in the boards.

Through it all, Marietta's door was kept closed, so that she would be disturbed as little as possible. Twice each week Mrs. Lenfesty came to see her daughter, but she drove over alone, much to Meg's disappointment.

Frequently, Meg took Marietta's trays to her at mealtime and tried to coax her to eat the broths and custards Tilda went to such pains to prepare.

On a Friday evening toward the end of September, Meg sat by the bedside while Marietta, propped up with pillows, toyed with the food before her.

"Why don't you taste that breast of chicken? Tilda fixed it special," Meg entreated the patient.

Marietta took a small bite. "Tell Tilda it is very nice, but I'm just not hungry. How is the housecleaning coming along?"

"Millie and I finished the parlor this afternoon. Carpet's down and curtains are back up. And that's the last of it, thank goodness!" Meg exclaimed, thinking that Marietta's face was very nearly as white as the pillows.

"I'm sorry I wasn't able to do my part. I feel pretty lazy just lying here. I think I'm finished with the food, Meg. Please put the tray on the dresser and then talk to me."

Meg complied with the first request, then returned to her chair. "Did you have a good visit with your mother this afternoon?"

"Yes. I wish Mama wouldn't worry so about me. She wants me to go to town and stay with Grandma, so Dr. Dixon can see me frequently until I get back on my feet again." Marietta traced the quilt pattern absent-mindedly with a thin forefinger.

"And are you going to?"

"I don't think Mike would want me to," she said slowly, then smiled faintly, "and it's a wife's duty to obey her husband, you know."

"But Marietta, surely Mike wants you well."

"He says I have everything I need right here. And he's right," she added a little wistfully.

But it doesn't keep you from longing for other things, Meg thought, such as a husband you can love and respect.

"Mama brought some Indianapolis newspapers. Calvin sent them," Marietta went on. "Why don't you read to me. I should know what's going on."

Meg took the papers from a chair and began scanning a front page for something that would interest her cousin's wife.

"Hmmm. There are columns and columns about some debates between two Illinois men running against each other for the senate, Stephen A. Douglas and Abraham Lincoln." Meg read silently for a moment. "Now why would an Indiana newspaper give so much space to something concerning Illinois?"

"I think it's because they are debating mostly about slavery, and that concerns the whole country," Marietta replied gravely.

"Here are a lot of quotations from other papers about it. Want me to read them?"

"Please do."

"Well, this one is from the Philadelphia *Press*. It says this about Mr. Lincoln: 'Poor fellow! He was writhing in the powerful grasp of Judge Douglas, an intellectual giant. Lincoln's speech amounted to nothing. . . . He was confused, and, after blundering along, . . . he sat down. Lincoln is the worst used up man in the United States.'" Meg paused and looked at Marietta. "They certainly don't think much of him, do they?"

"Probably a Democratic newspaper," Marrietta said. "Read some more."

"This is from the New York *Evening Post*." Meg read farther down the column. "'In repose Long Abe's appearance is not comely. But stir him up and the fire of genius plays on every feature. His eye glows and sparkles, every feature, now so ill formed, grows brilliant and expressive. . . . He is altogether a more fluent speaker than Douglas and in all the arts of debate fully his equal.'" Meg laughed. "I take it that that newspaper is published by Republicans. Here a Missouri newspaper calls Lincoln the Tall Sucker and Douglas the Little Giant. They must look queer together on a platform, the one so tall and the other so short."

"Any other news that's interesting?" Marietta asked.

"Well, here it tells about a ball at the governor's mansion in Indianapolis. And just think, he and his wife were right here at Sycamore Park last July!"

"That seems a long time ago, doesn't it?" Marietta sighed. "I think I'm tired now, Meg."

"All right, I'll leave you. Do you mind if I take these papers to my room and read them?" Meg put the newspapers under her arm and picked up the tray.

In her room Meg lighted a candle and read all the papers, even the text of the last Lincoln-Douglas debate in Illinois.

She learned that a new way of taking down speeches as men talked—shorthand writing—had been invented and the words of both men had been taken down verbatim.

On Sunday, Calvin attended church and afterward tied his saddle horse to the back of Meg's buggy and drove her to Sycamore Park.

"Pa's glad I decided to stay on the farm," he told her. "Says he'll deed forty acres to me when I get ready to settle down, and I know just the forty I want; right next to Mrs. Eakins' place on the Pike. You know where?"

"Yes, I know. Is it good land?"

"Mighty good and there's a piece of timberland with it to be cleared. The logs could be used for a house, in case I'd ever need one." Calvin glanced at Meg, then back at the horse. "How's Sis feeling."

"About the same. Doesn't eat enough to keep a bird alive. Uncle Barney and the others moved back to the house yesterday. We finished the fall cleaning Friday." Meg wished he would talk some more about the house he might be needing.

"With Mike back in the same house, she'll probably get worse. I wish we could get her out of there," he said unhappily.

"But there's no way. She's a Donahue now. Friday night I read her those newspapers you sent over." Meg decided she better introduce the subject if she expected to show off her knowledge.

Calvin brightened. "Good. I'm glad she felt like listening."

"Well, I didn't read very long to her. She soon got tired. But afterward I took them to my room and read every word."

"Good for you! Quite a ruckus those two are stirring up over in Illinois. I'd give most anything to hear one of those debates. I expect it would be quite a sight just to see the crowds that attend, too. I read that at one place, in August, twelve thousand gathered to hear them, and stood out in the broiling sun for three hours. I tell you those two have stirred people up, not just in Illinois, but all over the country. If Lincoln can just win that Senate seat, I predict he'll have a long political future." Sycamore Park came into view. Calvin shook his head. "I declare, it seems the distance from church is mighty short. I'm going to have to find a longer route."

Meg smiled. "October 2, next Saturday, is racing day," she informed him. "Had to postpone it, you know, when Jason was killed."

Calvin sobered. "I wish you didn't have to be close to all that. It's not right for a lady to be exposed to the things that go on here on a racing day."

"Don't worry. I'll stay close to the house. Ladies aren't invited to the fall races."

"Just the same, I wish——" He turned into the lane. At Meg's direction he headed toward the stables, where Jethro came out to unhitch for her.

Calvin helped her down from the buggy, untied his horse, mounted, and rode away.

"That Lenfesty boy is right smart of a fellow," Jethro remarked, unbuckling a strap at the shaft.

"Yes. He's going to be a farmer," Meg said, her eyes on the rider nearing the Pike.

"Well, whatever he sets out to do, I 'low as how he'll make a success at it. There's good blood in them Lenfestys." Jethro led the horse away.

Meg made her way up the hill. Forty acres on the Pike! It

would be a nice start for any man, and with the right wife to help him, a man could go far. But first a man had to ask, in order to get the right wife.

She sighed and took off her gloves as she mounted the steps to the porch.

Patience, Meg Donahue, she told herself.

XVI

GYPSY CURSE

October 2 was a beautiful Indian-summer day, warm, clear, and bright, the sky so blue that the trees, beginning to change colors, stood out against it in vivid silhouettes.

Meg finished her housework early so she could station herself on the front porch and watch the racing events at the track. It seemed to her that there was even a larger crowd than there had been in July, and certainly there were more Indians. It was easy to spot them because of their long hair, bright-colored calico shirts, and the fact that they rode without saddles, their feet hanging loose on either side of their mounts. Someday, Meg thought, she would like to visit the Indian village, about eight miles away.

She had lived here almost six months, and she thought of Cincinnati and Grandma less and less. "Young folks forget quickly," Grandma had told her once, "but the old remember and remember, till their last breath." Meg supposed that was because the best was behind the old ones, but her best lay before her, she was sure. Where would she be five years from now? In five years it would be 1863, and a lot could happen by then. Grandma had said it was fortunate that folks couldn't see into the future; if they could they wouldn't want to live, seeing all the heartbreak in store for them. But Meg felt that Grandma had been overly pessimistic. Sure, there would be bad things to live through, but there would be good ones too, and she, Meg, was ready to meet all that was in her future. And today there were those beautiful race horses to watch.

Racing day over, she settled down to a routine; housework in the morning, sit by Marietta's bed at noon while the invalid pretended to eat, then ride in the afternoon, ending up at the schoolhouse to take Lizzie home on Blackie's back.

Soon October had a nip in the air and nightly frosts turned the foliage to strong, rich reds, yellows, and browns. Meg felt that her eyes could not drink in enough of this natural miracle. Cincinnati was never like this.

On a Saturday, in the middle of the month, she rode farther than usual and found herself on River Road. She stopped at Mrs. Guthro's for a while to give the seamstress news of Marietta.

Then, riding on toward the river, Meg decided to go along the bank for a way. This river fascinated her with its lovely name, sounding like a whisper in the wind—Mississinewa. Jethro had told her about the savage Indian battles that had taken place along the Mississinewa right on this spot in 1812. It was hard to imagine such things happening here, it was so beautiful.

She tied Blackie to a tree, back from the river bank. Then, lifting her riding skirt in front, she climbed up on a promontory overlooking the river, and sat down.

The river wound its way, undulating over and around rocks, like a live thing. The trickling sound of the water, the riotous colors of the trees, the warmth of the sun, filled her with pleasure. What a marvel, October! It was so lovely it made her throat ache.

She wished that Calvin were here to enjoy this with her. It would be even more wonderful with him beside her. She hoped work had eased up on the Lenfesty farm and he could be at church tomorrow.

The shadows of the trees on the water were lengthening. She must leave. As she rose to her feet, she heard voices downriver, on the other side. Several Indian children ran out of a thicket. Meg stepped behind a bush to watch them at play. If they saw her, they might go away.

They threw stones in the water, and chased one another, shouting and laughing. An older girl, dressed in red calico, her hair in two long black braids, came out of the woods and spoke to them. They scattered back among the trees and left the girl alone.

Slowly the Indian girl edged her way out on a log that projected into the water. Turning her back toward Meg, she dropped something into the water. What was she doing? Meg wondered. She turned slightly and Meg saw that she was fishing, for at that moment she drew up a flopping fish on the end of a line. With the wriggling fish between her hands, the girl crept back on the log to the bank. She made a brilliant spot of color against the gray rocks on the shore.

Meg's attention was drawn from the opposite bank to movement downstream on her own side of the river. A horseman rode to the water's edge and his horse bent its neck to drink. Meg shrunk behind the bush, for the rider was Mike!

She glanced across the river. The Indian girl's head was bent over the fishhook as she put on fresh bait. Meg looked again at her cousin, now sitting straighter in the saddle as he too saw the girl.

Meg watched him bend, pull a rifle from the side of his saddle, put it to his shoulder, and take aim. She stifled a scream at the resounding shot and saw the figure in red on the opposite bank fall to the ground.

It wasn't real! It couldn't have happened! No one shot a defenseless girl in cold blood, not even Mike!

She saw Mike replace the rifle, pull his horse's head from the water, and continue along the bank.

Across the river two Indian men emerged from the thicket. One ran to the girl, the other watched Mike as he disappeared among the trees. The two picked up Mike's victim and carried her away.

It had happened so quickly that now, all out of sight, Meg wondered if she had imagined it. But across the way, the fish still flopped about on the bank and she knew that it was all too true.

Trembling, she mounted her horse and returned to Sycamore Park as fast as Blackie could take her.

The sun was disappearing by the time she got to the stables. Joey ran out to take Blackie.

"Where's Uncle Barney?" she asked as she slid from the saddle.

"Over talking to the blacksmith."

Meg ran quickly toward the blacksmith shop.

"Uncle Barney," she called as he came toward her. "I've got to tell you what I just saw."

Barney Donahue stopped beside her, his huge frame towering up at her side like a silo beside a corncrib.

"What's got you in such a tizzy?" he asked with a grin.

"I just saw Mike shoot an Indian girl over by the river!"

The grin disappeared from her uncle's face. "Keep your voice down," he ordered. "Now calm yourself and tell me about it."

Meg described the entire episode.

"Anyone else see it?"

"I don't know. Two men came and carried her away."

"Well, let's hope they didn't recognize Mike. Now you keep your mouth shut, you hear? I'll see Mike and maybe send him away for a while. He was a fool to do such a thing in broad day. He bought a new rifle yesterday and I reckon he wanted to try it out. That's Mike for you, shoot at anything he's a mind to."

"But Uncle Barney, shouldn't you notify the sheriff that there's been a murder? Won't Mike have to go to jail?"

"Oh tut, tut, that fiddle-faddle. It was only an Indian, and besides, you don't know she's dead."

"But Mike should be punished. That girl wasn't doing one single thing to him."

Barney Donahue took hold of Meg's shoulder and pressed his big hand hard into her flesh. "Meg Donahue, you're our kin and it's your bounden duty to keep mum. You start blabbing around and you'll find yourself in trouble. It's about time you realize which side your bread's buttered on. You go on to the house. And mind now, not a peep out of you. I'll look around for Mike."

Meg never knew how she got through the evening meal. The food tasted like sawdust; she was able to choke down only a few bites. Mike didn't come to supper. Meg wondered if he already had run away. Uncle Barney looked worried and as soon as he finished eating, he said to his four sons:

"Boys, I want you to light out and find Mike. I've got to talk to him."

"What's he been up to this time, Pa," Adelaide wanted to know.

"Oh, never you mind," Uncle Barney said, dismissing her.

That night, in bed, Meg tumbled and tossed, the tragedy on the river bank churning around and around in her mind like a side wheel on a river boat back in Cincinnati. If she could only quit thinking about it long enough to get to sleep.

She should never have come to Sycamore Park. Uncle Barney had threatened trouble if she told what she knew. What would he do to her? Shouldn't she ride into town tomorrow and report what she had seen to the sheriff? But if she did, would he do anything? Mrs. Guthro had said, "Around here the Donahues are the law."

What a position she was in! Surely she owed Uncle Barney a certain loyalty in return for all he had given her. But should that loyalty extend to concealing murder? Was ever a girl in such a dilemma! Her conscience writhed with its problem. If she told what she knew she would be disloyal to her benefactors, but if she didn't she would be disloyal to all that Grandma had taught her of right and wrong. She prayed for an answer, but none came.

Her restless sleep was filled with horrible dreams, dreams of Indians doing a war dance, of screaming children and, worst of all, of evil Mike Donahue.

Next morning she felt as limp as a dishrag, as Grandma used to say. She dressed for church. It would be good to get away from this house and into a church to pray further for guidance.

But Meg did not go to church. Just as she came out on the front porch, pulling on her gloves, Ross and Ben drove a wagon to the steps. After searching since dawn for their missing brother, they had brought him home. Uncle Barney and Todd brushed past Meg and down the steps to the wagon.

"He's dead, Pa," Ben said. "We found him by the river, shot and—and—scalped. No doubt about it. It was them red devils."

Todd looked in the wagon, then came back on the porch. "Meg, you better go back in. It's no sight for you. I expect you should break the news to Marietta." Todd opened the door for Meg. "I guess that long-ago gypsy curse has come true. He sure came to a bad end."

In the afternoon Meg saddled her horse and rode to the Lenfestys'. She told Marietta's family the whole sordid story.

Mrs. Lenfesty turned pale. "Well, thank God, my poor girl is rid of that fiend at last. How did she take it, Meg?"

"It's hard to say. She seemed sort of dazed, just laid there staring off into space as though her mind was miles away. I had thought she was some better; she'd had color in her cheeks."

"Yes, I noticed that the last time I saw her," Mrs. Lenfesty said, "but her cough seems just as bad."

Calvin stood up and ran his hand through his hair. "Pa, we must take Sis away from Sycamore Park. She's got no ties with the Donahues now. Let's take her into town to Grandma's, where Doc Dixon can keep an eye on her. That way she'll have a chance to be cured." He walked to Meg's chair and looked down. "And Meg, you must go to Grandma's too. You've got to get away from that family," he said grimly.

Meg hesitated, then stood up and looked around at the Lenfestys. "No. I'm going to stay at Sycamore Park. The Donahues are *my* family!"

Calvin was startled. "But you can't! It's no place for you! Those Donahues are no good! They're thieves and liars and now murderers." His face grew tense with indignant anger.

Meg flushed. "That may be true, but no matter what they've done, they took me in when I needed a home. I've made up my mind and I have to stay. Perhaps it's because of Todd, he's such a decent sort. Or maybe it's because of Adelaide, she's really sort of pitiful. But anyway, I just know I can't move out, now that they're in bad trouble."

Calvin's eyes narrowed. He put his hands on Meg's shoulders and gave her a shake. "Meg Donahue, you don't know what you're talking about! You're not old enough to judge what's best for you!"

Meg drew away from him. "Let loose of me, Calvin! I'm too old to let you dictate to my conscience. I've had enough trouble with it as it is. And now that I've made up my mind, you can't change it."

"But Meg——" Calvin's anger turned to bewilderment. "Think of what they've done to Marietta. You don't belong there."

"Calvin," Mrs. Lenfesty interrupted, "let her alone. I can well imagine what a strain you've been under, Meg, torn in all directions. It's probably right for you to stick by your kinfolks. A person must do some things, no matter what."

Blackie had to pick his own way back to Sycamore Park, for Meg's eyes were too full of tears to see the road. She knew she had lost Calvin. He just couldn't understand why she was sticking by Uncle Barney. In fact, she scarcely understood it herself. Uncle Barney was all that Calvin had said, a man with no sense of integrity at all; but, he had taken her in. However, she mustn't fool herself. She could not hope to change the order of things at Sycamore Park. She could not undo evil. Then why had she chosen to remain? It would be so easy to go into Rollins with Marietta and live with respectable Grandma Lenfesty. What was the inner pull that made her resist Calvin's orders?

She had felt for some time that Calvin was on the verge of proposing to her. All that talk about whether he should work in town or on the farm and about the forty acres his father was going to deed to him and the house that he would build there. A girl could sense what a man had on his mind. But now that she had defied his wishes, she was sure he would think differently. A man didn't want a girl who wouldn't obey him.

And yet, if he really loved her——!

She shivered as she climbed the steps of the front porch at Sycamore Park, thinking of the horrors she had witnessed in the last two days. Inside, in the hall, she glanced into the sitting room and saw Adelaide seated and staring into the flames of the fireplace.

Meg hesitated a moment, then went in. The older woman did not move. Meg touched her shoulder lightly. "Are you all right, Adelaide?"

Adelaide raised her head, then shook it slowly. "It's been years since I've been all right, Meg. You told the Lenfestys?" Meg nodded. "What did they say? Glad, I suppose, that their daughter is free of him at last."

"They are going to take Marietta into town on Tuesday. She'll go to her grandmother's, so she can be near the doctor."

Adelaide nodded. "That's good. That poor girl is in a bad way, I'm afraid." She looked up at Meg. "And you, you'll be going with her, I presume."

"No, Adelaide. I'm staying here, if you still want me."

"But I thought, well I got the impression that you and Marietta's brother——" Adelaide stood up, put her hands on Meg's shoulders, and looked down into her eyes. "Meg, your coming here has been the one good thing that ever happened to this house. Of course I want you, and—and need you."

"But Adelaide, you never acted as though you did." Meg thought she saw moisture in her cousin's eyes.

"I know. Ever since Mama died I've made a kind of hard shell around myself in order to keep going. Any show of softness and Pa and my brothers might have destroyed me, I expect. Todd has been my one hope. You have lived here long enough, Meg, to know what we're like. Pa and the boys are not likely to change. But you can be a great comfort to *me*."

Monday morning the Donahue brothers buried Mike next to Jason, and in the afternoon Adelaide and Meg packed Marietta's clothes.

From her window, the following day, Meg watched Calvin

and his father drive up in a big wagon. She hurried to Marietta's room.

"They're here," she said, picking up a wool scarf from the foot of the bed. "I'll put this on your head."

Marietta touched Meg's hand. "Meg, you will come in to see me?"

"Of course. And you'll soon be a lot better with the doctor seeing you every day." Meg tied the scarf under Marietta's chin.

"I'm glad you will be here with Adelaide. She needs you, Meg." Marietta stuck out a foot and Meg put a wool stocking on it. "She's had a hard life. And she did what she could for me." She stuck out the other foot. "And Todd, Meg, he's as honest as the day. I hope he can stay that way."

Meg helped Marietta into a wool dressing gown. "I know. He's been very kind to me." Meg unfolded a comforter and spread it on one side of the bed.

Adelaide entered at that point, followed by Calvin. Meg avoided his eyes as he approached the bed.

"Calvin," Adelaide directed, "put her onto that comforter and we'll wrap it around her."

Calvin lifted his frail sister gently. "There you are, Sis," he said, helping Adelaide tuck the coverlet about the patient. "We've got more covers in the wagon. I don't think you'll feel a mite of cold." He picked her up and made his way to the door, not looking once at Meg.

Meg stood at the top of the stairs and watched them descend. She returned to her room and looked out the window.

Tilda and Millie were below, bidding Marietta farewell. Meg saw them wipe their eyes as Mr. Lenfesty and Calvin placed the girl on a pallet in the wagon bed. Adelaide reached in and patted Marietta's shoulder.

Meg felt her own eyes fill with tears. Maybe Marietta had a chance to get well now that Mike was gone. How glad she must be to leave this house and all the pain she had suffered here. Now, Meg supposed, she would never learn why Marietta had come here in the first place.

She watched the wagon drive away. Would she ever see Calvin again? He hadn't spoken to her. Had she been wrong to ignore his demand, wrong to remain at Sycamore Park?

"Good-by, Cal Lenfesty," she whispered, "good-by. I think I might have loved you."

XVII

MARIETTA'S SECRET

In the days that followed, Adelaide seemed to Meg to be a different person. The wretched deaths of her two brothers weighed heavily upon her. In fact, all of the Donahues went around with somber faces, saying very little.

When Meg spoke of it to Millie, Millie replied, "And well they might be down in the mouth. It's just beginning to dawn on 'em that the wages of sin is death!"

Meg helped Adelaide clean Marietta's room, but Adelaide's heart wasn't in it. Even housecleaning had lost savor. Climbing on a chair to take down the curtains, Adelaide said, "You know, Meg, I could have made things easier for Marietta if I had just had the gumption to stand up to Mike and Pa. But I guess it's too late to be sorry now."

"Marietta said you had been good to her."

"Did she? Well, she's the kind that speaks well of everyone. I could have done a heap more. When you go in to see her, I want to send her something nice."

Early in November, the day after election, the male Donahues became even more "down in the mouth."

"It's because Sheriff Ramsey got beat," Todd told Meg when she questioned him. "Dan Cochran is the new sheriff. Guess Pa thinks he won't be so friendly to us Donahues."

Meg wondered what would happen if the new sheriff found out about the counterfeit money. He wouldn't take office until after the new year, but he might be looking into the county's affairs even now. And if he discovered the kind of transactions that went on at the cabin on the creek, what would he do? She was a part of this family; would she be held accountable for the misdemeanors perpetrated by the others?

Well, that was the chance she took when she put her lot in with them. But she wasn't sorry. Only, she thought a little wistfully, it would be nice to talk to Calvin about politics or slavery or—or his forty acres, or to watch the comet with him again. But, with Marietta gone, she didn't feel free to ride to the Lenfesty farm. Calvin had been so angry with her. And, she thought testily, he had shaken her like a child! He had to understand that she was a Donahue with a mind of her own! It was right that she behave honorably toward her family, even if they were unworthy of her loyalty. She had to be true to herself, even if she did make Calvin angry.

Shortly after election day, Meg and Adelaide sat in the sitting room sewing. Meg worked on quilt pieces while Adelaide stitched on a flannel bed jacket for Marietta.

"When I finish this, maybe you'll take it to her for me," Adelaide said, threading her needle with pink thread.

"Why don't you take it yourself?" Meg asked.

"No. I'm sure the Lenfestys wouldn't want me. It's better if they aren't reminded of Mike." Adelaide took a tiny stitch on the garment.

Before Meg could urge further, the big knocker on the front door sounded with a loud rap.

"See who that is, will you please, Meg?" Adelaide asked.

Meg opened the door to Joyce. "Oh, Meg, I'm glad *you* came to the door. I would have died if it had been one of the others."

"It's good to see you, Joyce, come in. I've gone to church every Sunday, but none of you were ever there." Meg opened the door wider and Joyce stepped in.

"We've been at Grandma's every Sunday to spend the day with Marietta," Joyce replied.

Meg took Joyce into the sitting room, where Adelaide greeted the girl kindly.

"Marietta asked me to come," Joyce explained. "She wishes you would come to see her, Meg."

"She does?" Meg hesitated. "I—I wasn't sure your grandmother would want me."

"Of course she does. We all do."

Meg pointed to the pink bed jacket in Adelaide's hands. "Adelaide's making a jacket for Marietta. As soon as she finishes it, I'll take it in."

Adelaide cut a thread. "I should finish it tonight," she said. "How's Marietta?"

"Well, Mama thinks she looks some better, but it seems to me she coughs an awful lot. Dr. Dixon says if she can just maintain her strength through the winter, she'll show great improvement come spring."

Meg wanted to ask about Calvin, but she avoided the subject. Joyce rose to go and Meg accompanied her to the door.

"Where did you leave your buggy?" Meg asked, looking out as she opened the door.

"Why, down on the Pike," Joyce replied, slightly embarrassed. "Cal's waiting down there. He drove me over."

Meg's hand tightened on the doorknob. "I see."

"Oh, Meg, what's happened? You and Cal were getting on so well. I thought if I got him to bring me over here, he'd come in with me. But he was so stubborn, just sat in the buggy and refused to budge." Joyce's face showed distress.

"Don't fret yourself, Joyce. Your brother's actions don't bother me at all. I don't know why he got so huffy just because I chose to be with my family. Maybe he's beginning to realize that I'm a wild Donahue too."

"Meg! You're not! And you know it. Marietta says you are one of the nicest girls she has ever met. And I know it too. I don't understand why you want to line yourself up with Barney Donahue and his sons. Oh, Meg, why don't you leave this place? Papa says it's doomed." Joyce looked earnestly into Meg's face.

Meg shook her head and tightened her lips. "I'm a Donahue, Joyce. I belong here, doomed or not."

She watched Joyce run down the hill toward the Pike. Slowly she returned to the sitting room and picked up a quilt block. Probably she would never see Calvin again.

The next day at noon, Meg saddled her horse and rode to town carrying Adelaide's bed jacket and some special food Millie and Tilda had prepared for Marietta.

Meg's diffidence at calling at the Lenfestys' was soon dispelled by Marietta's grandmother.

"Thank you for coming, Meg. She's looked for you every day."

Mrs. Lenfesty took the food to the kitchen while Meg mounted the stairs with Adelaide's package. She went into the room Mrs. Lenfesty had designated.

Marietta's hand was over her eyes. Meg tiptoed to the foot of the bed, wondering if she were asleep. There had been a great change, Meg thought, in the few weeks since she had last seen the patient. Her figure seemed so slight under the covers and the hand over her eyes was thin and transparent.

Marietta removed the hand, saw Meg, and smiled.

"I'm glad it's you, Meg. How are you? Take off your hat and sit here beside me."

Meg complied and handed over the package. Marietta opened it and exclaimed at Adelaide's kindness. Meg helped her put on the jacket. She lay back on her pillow and touched the pink bow at her throat.

It was strange, Meg thought, that even after her long illness, Marietta was still beautiful—if anything, even more so than before. Dark curls framed her delicate face, her eyes were deep and luminous, and the pink of her cheeks made the bed jacket seem pale.

"You look so pretty, Marietta. Wish I could paint a picture of you. You're like the pink apple blossoms that bloom in the spring at Sycamore Park. Remember how lovely they are?"

Marietta nodded, put out her hand, and touched Meg's arm. "Yes, I remember. But let's not talk about spring. I wanted you to come, Meg, because I couldn't bring myself to speak to the others. You see, dear, I'm reasonably sure that I'll never see another spring."

Meg's eyes widened and stung with quick tears as she took Marietta's hand. "Oh, please don't say that! You're getting better. Everyone says so."

"Now don't fret yourself, Meg. Of course, no one knows when his time will come. But I feel that mine is near. And I want you to tell the others after I'm gone that it's all right; that in fact I am quite happy about it. Maybe if they know, it will comfort them, especially Mama."

"But Marietta, now that Mike's gone, there's a real chance for a good life ahead for you." Meg wished Grandma Lenfesty would come in. This talk of death was something she scarcely knew how to handle.

Marietta smiled sadly. "There were times at Sycamore Park when I wanted to die. But it was not to be. My life ended when I lost the chance to marry the man I loved. And Meg, when I am gone I want you to tell my family why I married Mike Donahue. But until then will you keep the secret?"

Meg left the chair and sat on the edge of the bed. "Of course, Marietta. Mrs. Guthro told me about John Parrish and your wedding plans."

"Dear Mrs. Guthro—she was the last to see me a happy normal person. I remember that day perfectly, Meg. I had tried on my wedding dress at her house; it was almost finished. As I rode away I was dreaming of the light in John's eyes when he would see me in it on our wedding day." Marietta turned her head away and Meg saw a tear glide down the young woman's cheek. Meg took a handkerchief and wiped it away.

"Perhaps you would rather not go on now," she suggested.

"No, dear, I must tell you. They were waiting for me farther along on River Road, Mike and his brothers, all but Todd. Mike told me they knew the exact whereabouts of John and that unless I married him, Mike, right then, they would hunt John down and kill him." Marietta clasped the bedcovers tightly and her cheeks grew brighter. "I had no choice, Meg. I knew they would do as they threatened. They had killed others who got in the way of what they wanted. I saved John, but when I married Mike I was lost forever."

Meg took Marietta's hand. "Marietta, I think John Parrish may have been at Sycamore Park last September." She related her meeting with Jay Parridon, describing him and telling of his questions about Marietta. "So you see, he is still interested in your welfare. Why can't I write a letter to him for you, telling of Mike's death and that you did it all to save him? He could come to see you now."

"No, no. It wouldn't be safe. The Donahues would be sure to be on hand to do away with Jason's killer. I would not have him run the risk." Marietta looked toward the window. "I never expect to see John in this world. But Meg, if I don't get well, will you tell Mama I'd like to be buried in my wedding dress? Mrs. Guthro still has it."

Meg's eyes filled with tears. "Now, Marietta, don't talk like that. You'll be up and around come spring. Maybe you'll come out to Sycamore Park and see the orchards in bloom."

Marietta gave a long sigh and smiled gently. "You may be right."

Meg rose. "You're tired. I'd better go."

"I am, a little. But I'm glad someone knows. It's worried me that I had told no one. Thank Adelaide for the jacket. She's a good soul, really. I'm glad you're out there with her. She and Todd need you."

"Calvin thinks I should be here with you," Meg blurted out.

Marietta raised her eyebrows. "So—that's what's bothering him! I'll have a talk with him. He worries about you, Meg."

"Well, he needn't. I can look out for myself."

"Of course you can. Come back soon, dear, when it's convenient."

Downstairs, Meg longed to tell Grandma Lenfesty of the conversation, but she must keep Marietta's secret. She held back her tears until she was in the saddle, and then they coursed down her cheeks steadily.

She dried her eyes when she reached the Pike, and wished there was someone with whom she might share Marietta's story. Was she really that ill—ill enough to die? Did her family suspect the seriousness of her condition? Well, she must not tell them. Let them hope as long as they could. A year ago, little did she dream the tests she would be put to.

The most difficult thing about living at Sycamore Park, Meg thought, was squaring her thinking about sin and retribution. She had been taught that sin and evil did not pay, that sinners were always punished. And yet there was Uncle Barney's family living in luxury and not suffering at all for the meanness they committed.

But, on second thought, that wasn't quite so. There was Mike! He certainly came to a bad end, and Jason too. Would the others have to pay in like manner? Well, she must trust the Lord. Punishment was not in her hands. Retribution might be a long time coming, but she felt it was inevitable.

In the meantime, she must do what she could for Adelaide and Todd. Marietta thought she had been right to stay at Sycamore Park.

If only Calvin could see it that way. Why did he have to be so bullheaded?

Jethro approached her as she put Blackie in his stall.

"Miss Meg, could I speak to you?"

Meg held her riding skirt up at the side, off the barn floor. "Anything wrong?" she asked, seeing him look furtively about.

"I found three folks hidin' in the cow barn a while ago. Mrs. Marietta used to help the likes of 'em on their way, but now—— What do you think I ought to do. If Barney found 'em he'd turn 'em in sure as shootin'."

Meg thought quickly. "Oh, no. Don't tell Uncle Barney. I'll think of something. Are they up in the haymow?"

"Yes. A woman, a boy, and a girl. They're safe for the time being. But they'll need something to eat."

"I'll take them some food and try to decide what's best to do. I've just come from seeing Marietta. I know she'd want us to help them."

Jethro nodded. "How is the little lady?"

"She's pretty sick, Jethro, I'm afraid."

"I calculated she wasn't long for this world the last time I seen her. Well, let me know if there's anything I can do for them runaways."

Meg managed to filch a loaf of bread from the pantry and a pitcher of milk from the milkhouse. She climbed the ladder to the haymow in the cow barn, and after several whispered assurances that she was a friend, the three crept out of the hay and took the food. Meg told them to stay hidden and she would come for them later.

In her room she lighted the lamp and removed her riding habit. What should she do now? If Calvin were alerted, she could take them to meet him on River Road, as she had before. But he didn't know. She knew of no way to get to the Lenfestys' except on the Pike, and she couldn't run the risk of asking Uncle Barney for a wagon in which to transport the runaways. Should she ride Blackie over there after supper?

She pulled a dress over her head, smoothed her hair, and hurried down to the dining room.

Uncle Barney, Ben, Chris, and Ross listened as Todd and Adelaide questioned her about Marietta.

"She's very sick," Meg told them.

Uncle Barney cleared his throat. "Addie, next time you go to town I want you to buy some nice goods for a fine dress and take it to Marietta from me. Get the best they got."

Adelaide shook her head. "You're a little late with kindness, Pa. I'm afraid that girl will never wear another dress except the one she'll be buried in."

Uncle Barney stood up and pounded the table. "You do as I say, Addie. You go to town tomorrow. You hear?"

Adelaide sighed. "Very well, Pa, if it'll soothe your conscience any. But it would have been a sight better if you had whaled the daylights out of Mike when he used to be so mean to her."

Uncle Barney stomped from the room followed by his three older sons. Adelaide looked at Meg, shrugged her shoulders, and went to the kitchen.

Todd pushed back his chair. "Next time I'm in town I'll go see her. Do you think the Lenfestys would mind?"

"Oh, do go, Todd. They'd want you to. Marietta is so fond of you." Meg looked at him. Marietta trusted Todd. Did she dare take him into her confidence about the three in the barn? "Todd, would you like to do something for Marietta?"

"You know I would, Meg."

"Well," Meg hesitated a moment, then lauched into an account of Marietta's part in the secret passage of runaway slaves through this part of Indiana. She told how she herself had assisted last July on racing day. And now, not knowing that Marietta was gone, three had found their way here and were hiding in the cow barn.

Todd leaned an elbow on the table. "So? And we need to get them out of there and on to the next place, is that it?"

"Yes. If Calvin just knew about them, he'd take them to the next station."

"Well, why don't I take them over to the Lenfesty farm tonight and turn them over to Calvin?"

"Oh Todd, would you? Can you do it without the others knowing?"

"Sure. The Donahues are noted for sly dealings. It's about time one of us did a good deed for a change."

And so it was that around midnight Meg went to the cow barn, wakened the three in the haymow, and helped them cover up with straw in the back of the wagon Todd had driven to the barn door.

"Thank you, Todd," she whispered as he took up the reins.

"You get along to bed," he urged. "It's late for you to be out, Cousin Meg." He leaned down and patted her arm. "These folks will be all right. I'll get them to Calvin."

From her window she watched the wagon disappear into the shadows of the night.

XVIII

NOT TO BE MARRIED IN

It was late next morning when Todd came downstairs.

"How did things go last night?" Meg asked him.

"Right as rain. Didn't have any trouble at all rousing the Lenfestys. I think they were some surprised, however, to see *me* there on such an errand, especially Calvin. I told him that it was you who had engineered the whole thing."

"What did he say?" Meg asked, following her cousin into the dining room.

"He said it was lucky for those folks that you were around to see after them. I told him we were *all* lucky to have you around. Mrs. Lenfesty asked about you, said Joyce wished you'd come over, and that they all missed you. How come you *don't* go over there anymore?" Todd pulled a chair out at the table and sat down.

"Oh, I don't know. Marietta not living here and all—I—I, well I just thought——" She ended lamely.

"I think the next time I see Calvin I better have a talk with him. I expect he needs to be set straight on a few things. He should know that you're not a part of what goes on around here. Pa's reputation shouldn't be held against you."

"No, I'd rather you didn't say anything to Calvin." Meg walked to the door. "I'll go tell Millie to bring your breakfast."

When Meg returned from the kitchen, Todd was standing at the window looking toward the Pike.

"I suppose Calvin is on the road now, taking those people to the next place," he said contemplatively. "That's a fine thing the Lenfestys are doing. Why, do you know they have a room right off their kitchen with several cots in it where they bed the runaways! Guess they just keep it for that purpose. And Mrs. Lenfesty sat them down at the table and cooked for them while I was there, right in the middle of the night." Todd glanced around the large dining room and gave a humorless laugh. "And look at us, with this great big house! What do we do for folks? Not a plague-take-it thing!"

"You gave me a home," Meg reminded him.

"Yes." Todd put a hand on her shoulder. "You are our one good deed, Meggy, but you have repaid us and then some."

Meg shook her head. "There's little I can do for any of you. You have everything."

Todd looked into her eyes. "We have everything, Meg, and yet we have nothing. I thought when Marietta came here things would change, that Mike might be different with such a girl as his wife. But if anything, he was more of a devil than ever."

Meg pitied him, seeing the misery in his face. She was glad he wasn't aware of how Mike had accomplished that marriage.

Millie brought Todd's breakfast in and placed it on the table.

Snow piled on snow during December, changing Sycamore Park into a place of immaculate beauty. Every morning as soon as the men shoveled paths, Meg went to the stables to see Blackie. Often Adelaide accompanied her, carrying sugar for her own brown mare, Harriet.

It was Meg who suggested that they make a nice Christmas for Lizzie Ridenour. Adelaide knitted her a hood with mittens to match. Meg made the little girl a rag doll like the one Grandma Hartman had made her many years before. And Todd built a sled. Christmas afternoon Meg and Lizzie coasted down the hill in front of the house.

The winter wore on. Meg finished her quilt blocks and sewed them together. Adelaide said they'd get the quilting frames in soon and do the quilting. Jethro and Joey were on the move every day to keep the wood boxes filled and the fireplaces blazing. Chairs and settees were drawn near the fires in each room, for the edges of the rooms were very chilly. Meg taught Lizzie how to make hairpin lace during the week the snow was too deep for the child to go to school.

Uncle Barney, Ross, Ben, and Chris only ate and slept at the big house now. Meg wondered what they did all day at the stables and jockey house. It seemed as though since Mike's death they hadn't felt at ease in the big house.

Often Meg thought of Calvin and made up her mind that as soon as enough snow melted she would ride to the Lenfesty farm and inquire about Marietta. Oh, if only spring would come!

On a late afternoon the last week in February it got colder and snowed again. The light faded and Meg put aside the rag rug she was braiding and got up to light a lamp. She went to the sitting-room window and looked out.

Large snowflakes fluttered to the ground in the gray dusk, swirled occasionally by sudden gusts of wind. Meg shivered, feeling icy drafts seep in through the cracks. She couldn't see the Pike from here, but halfway up the lane a sleigh was approaching and now she could hear the bells. The vehicle passed the stables and came on to the house, stopping in front.

Adelaide was in bed with a cold, so Meg went to the door. She peered through a window in the hall and watched a man get out of the sleigh and walk slowly up the steps. Briefly

Meg's heart pounded in her ears. Even in the half-dark she recognized the broad shoulders.

Before the visitor had a chance to raise the knocker, Meg opened the door.

"Come in," she said, outwardly calm, as though they had spoken only yesterday. "Come in, it is very cold."

Calvin stomped the snow from his boots, stepped in, and removed his knitted cap. "Meg—Meg—I've come to tell you——" His voice choked and Meg knew, even before he said the words, what he had come to say. "It's Marietta. She's gone."

Meg couldn't see his face, for the house was almost dark now, only a flickering light playing out across the floor through the sitting-room door.

"Come in here," she said softly. "I'll light a lamp."

In the lamplight she looked up into his grief-stricken face. "When did it happen?"

"Early this morning. Mama sent me here, said you'd want to know. Oh, Meg," he burst out, "she was so fond of you. She's been after me all these weeks to come to see you, to get things right between us. I had no right to get my back up at you for wanting to stick by your folks. And now, here I put off seeing you, and it's too late. Marietta won't know that I've come at last." He searched his pockets for a handkerchief and blew his nose.

Meg's eyes filled with tears. "I'm sure she knows." She touched his arm comfortingly. "She talked to me last November about being gone by spring. Said you and your folks mustn't be sad. And Calvin, she wanted to be buried in her wedding dress, the one Mrs. Guthro still has. Will you tell your mother?"

Calvin looked down at Meg, then at the cap in his hand. "Do you suppose you could go back with me to Grandma's and stay until after the funeral. I think if you told Mama what Marietta said, it might comfort her."

Meg hesitated briefly, then said decisively, "Of course I'll go if you think I can help."

Todd came through the back hall and stood in the sitting-room doorway.

"Todd, Calvin came to tell us that Marietta's gone, passed away this morning."

Todd approached Calvin and held out his hand. "I'm sorry. She was a lovely girl. The world won't see the likes of her again. She meant a lot to me."

Calvin shook the proffered hand. "Thank you, Todd. She spoke often of you and your kindness to her."

"Todd, Calvin thinks I can be of some help to his mother. I'll go tell Adelaide and get my things." At the door she paused and looked back at the two young men. "Why don't you take Calvin to the kitchen, so he can tell Millie and Tilda. They loved Marietta so."

"Sure, Meg. Take off your coat, Calvin, and I'll put it in the hall." Todd smiled reassuringly at Meg.

It was only after Meg and Calvin were skimming over the hard-packed snow on the Pike toward Mrs. Guthro's that she remembered that it was nearly suppertime and she had not offered Calvin any food. When she mentioned it, he replied that he wasn't hungry; in fact, hadn't been all day.

At the tollgate Meg went in to tell Mrs. Eakins the sad news, also to mention that the funeral would be in town day after tomorrow and would Mrs. Eakins give the word to all passers-by?

"I'll see that everybody knows about it," the old lady answered. "It sure is a pity she had to be taken. But she'll be right at home up there in heaven, that girl; she was such an angel, good clean through, that's what she was." Mrs. Eakins wiped her eyes. "I see you're riding with Calvin. You and him made up?"

Meg was startled. "Why Mrs. Eakins, how did you know that——"

The tollgate keeper nodded and pursed her lips. "Not much I don't catch onto sooner or later around here. Calvin's a nice boy, Meg. And if you're smart you'll set your cap for him. You know what he's been doing all winter?" Meg shook her head. "He's been clearing the timber on that land of his next to mine and hauling the logs to the high spot yon side. Nice place up there for a little cabin, I'd say. A young couple can be mighty happy in a little place of their own. But then maybe you wouldn't be interested, seeing as how you live in such a fine place already."

Meg glanced into the sharp eyes and gave a quick smile. "I expect I could be persuaded to leave Sycamore Park if the right person asked me."

As they rode beyond the tollgate, Meg looked at the snow-covered fields along the Pike—Calvin's land. He said nothing, so she too remained silent. Perhaps Mrs. Eakins was wrong; he might just be felling that timber to sell. She settled back in the fur robe and thought of Marietta. She must be glad that the two of them were riding on the Pike together to do this one last errand for her.

Mrs. Guthro wept at their revelation and sobbed as she took the wedding dress from the chest.

"Oh, that dear angel! I had a premonition when I was making this dress; thought to myself, Not to be married in, but to be buried in." She wrapped the dress in a sheet and handed it to Calvin. "I'll come in town early tomorrow. I want to help lay out that dear girl." She opened the big book on the table. "I'm going to cut this page from my Bible, the page John Parrish wrote on. I think it should be buried with her."

Meg was told that it was the biggest funeral ever to take place in Rollins. People came from all over the county to pay their last respects to the beautiful Mrs. Mike Donahue, lying there in her white satin wedding dress.

Adelaide, Todd, Jethro, Millie, and Tilda came. Meg supposed Uncle Barney and his other sons hadn't the courage to put in an appearance, considering all the misery they had caused Marietta.

After the service at the cemetery, Joyce turned to Meg. "Do you suppose you could go home with us? You've been the only one able to give Mama any comfort. And once we get home I expect she'll feel worse than ever."

Meg nodded. "I'll go tell Adelaide." She made her way across the crusted snow to her two cousins, standing at the edge of the crowd.

"Adelaide, Joyce wants me to go home with them, just for tonight. Thinks I might be able to help Mrs. Lenfesty."

Adelaide patted Meg's arm. "Of course. I only wish I could do something for her. Going home after a funeral is the hard part." Adelaide's voice was hoarse from her cold.

"Todd, you see that Adelaide goes right to bed. All this raw air hasn't done that cold any good. I'll be home tomorrow." Meg pulled Adelaide's coat collar up in the back to shield her neck. "I expect you shouldn't have come out at all," she added concernedly.

Adelaide smiled appreciatively. "Don't worry about me, dear. Though I must say it's nice to have you care."

"Want me to come over after you tomorrow?" Todd asked.

"Oh, would you?"

"Sure. I'll be over in the afternoon sometime. All right?" Meg nodded and joined Joyce.

At the Lenfestys' they found that the neighbors had filled the pantry with food. Meg had never seen such an array: pies, cakes, roast chickens, baked hams, stewed chicken and dumplings, and fresh bread. Supper was on the table and serveral of the ladies stayed to serve the sorrowing family and to clean up the kitchen afterward.

Neighborliness was at its best during a family's bereavement, Meg noted.

After supper Mrs. Lenfesty wanted to talk about Marietta. She hunted all the pictures she had of her deceased daughter, to show Meg. The rest of the family left them together by the fire in the parlor. Meg listened and asked questions, urging the mother to relate incidents in Marietta's childhood. She remembered Grandma saying, "There's nothing like getting things out in the open and talked about to comfort a body. It's when you bottle them up inside you that you suffer and die a little."

When the fire had burned down to a red glow, Mrs. Lenfesty rose and put the albums on the table. She stood beside Meg's chair and rubbed her hand across the girl's shoulders. "You are a very understanding girl, Meg. I'm so glad you were there at Sycamore Park with Marietta. You made those last months easier for her." She wiped her eyes. "And now I suppose we'll never know why she did it—why she married Mike. My poor darling girl!" Mrs. Lenfesty sat down and wept again.

As Meg put out a comforting hand, she thought, I'll never tell Marietta's secret. The truth about that elopement would only cause her mother more suffering than she could bear. I must never tell. Marietta will understand.

XIX

"AS YE SOW"

Meg shared Joyce's room that night and the two exchanged many confidences before they slept.

It was in the dark hours before dawn that they were wakened by barking dogs. Joyce sat up in bed.

"Meg, something's wrong. Prince and Ned never bark like that without reason." Joyce ran to the window. "Someone just rode in."

The girls heard Mr. Lenfesty in the upstairs hall and then on the stairs. Joyce opened the door a crack as Meg joined her to listen. Shivering in their nightgowns, they heard only a faint mumble as the front door downstairs was opened briefly, then closed. Mr. Lenfesty came upstairs quickly and knocked at Calvin's door.

"Get up, Cal," Meg heard him say. "There's a big fire over at Sycamore Park! We'd best get over and help!"

Meg clutched Joyce's arm. "Fire! Oh, dear!" She turned away and began feeling for her clothes on the chair in the corner. "I've got to go too. Joyce, could you light a candle or the lamp? Oh, where did I put my shoes and stockings?"

Never had Meg Donahue dressed so quickly. She heard Calvin and Mr. Lenfesty going downstairs just as she tucked her hair into its net. Grabbing her coat and hood, she was out of the room and after them, Joyce holding the lamp high at the top of the stairs.

In the barn she found the two men saddling horses by lantern light. "Saddle a horse for me too," she told them determinedly.

Calvin looked up as he tightened his saddle. "But Meg——" He hesitated, then turned to his father. "She can ride Joyce's Charlie, can't she? Where's Joyce's saddle?"

"I don't know." Mr. Lenfesty glanced at Meg doubtfully. "You should have stayed in bed, Meg."

"Don't bother about hunting Joyce's saddle. Just get me any kind of saddle. I'll manage." She went to Charlie's stall and led the horse out.

Calvin took a saddle from the wall and fastened it on without protest. Meg put her foot in a stirrup and swung the other leg over as though she had been riding astride from the beginning. Her full skirts billowed out around her. Mr. Lenfesty watched the proceedings, blew out the lantern, mounted his horse, and the three rode out of the barn.

"We'll have to go by the Pike, Pa. Snow's still too deep for the short cut," Calvin said as they went along the lane. "How're you getting along, Meg."

"First rate. Much easier to ride this way."

"Who brought the news, Pa?"

"One of the men from Sycamore Park. It's the stables. They think someone set them on fire."

Meg caught her breath. The stables! O dear God! All those horses! And Blackie! Her Blackie! She dug her heels into Charlie's sides and bent over the saddle.

They galloped along the Pike at a fast clip. Other riders had joined them by the time they reached the tollgate. The gate was up; Mrs. Eakins, standing near by, waved them through like a general urging soldiers to battle.

Even before they passed the jockey house Meg could see the flames lighting the horizon. Oh, poor Adelaide, she thought, so miserable with a cold. What if the flames spread to the house? There was a slight wind. Might it not carry a spark to the roof? Was Sycamore Park really doomed?

All the riders dismounted at the lane entrance and tied their horses to the fence along the Pike. Meg followed Calvin and the others. The soaring flames made it as light as day and the crackling of the timbers sounded like pistol shots. As Meg came nearer the burning buildings, an acrid odor filled her nostrils.

"Just smell that!" a man cried. "Guess they didn't get all the horses out."

Meg put her hand to her mouth to stifle a cry. Calvin turned and took her arm. "You go on up to the house, Meg," he said, close to her ear to be heard in the din all about. "Adelaide will need you."

"Oh, Calvin, isn't there anything we can do?" She saw the flames through a blur of tears.

"Not much. All the stables will go, I'm afraid. They haven't even started a bucket brigade. Can't, I suppose, since the water in the creek is frozen solid. But look, over there. See, they did save some horses. Maybe——"

At that moment a man brushed by Meg's arm. She reached out her hand. "Oh, Jethro, are you all right? Where are Todd and Uncle Barney?"

The old man looked into her face, his own streaked with black, his clothes smelling of smoke.

"Miss Meg, ain't it awful?" His voice cracked. "We done our best, but we couldn't get 'em all out. Some of 'em burned to a crisp, poor critters." He gave a short sob. "But we got your black one. I led him out myself. He's safe and sound. Howsomever, Miss Adelaide's Harriet is gone. Mr. Todd himself got a bad burn trying to lead that mare out, but she wouldn't budge. You ought to go up to the house and comfort poor Miss Adelaide. She's in a bad way, I 'spect."

Meg turned to Calvin, rested her head on his shoulder, and cried bitterly.

He held her gently. "There, there, Meggy. Pull yourself together. Jethro's right, Adelaide needs you. Go on now."

Meg wiped her eyes on her sleeve, worked her way through the growing crowd of spectators, and climbed the hill to the house, swallowing hard all the way to get the ache from her throat.

She lifted her head. Lights streamed from every window in the house at the top of the hill, just as they had the first time she had seen it. The house looked the same, Meg thought, but she, herself, was not the same girl Jethro had driven up to that front door so many months ago. Or at least she didn't feel so. Maybe in fighting to keep her faith and integrity amid the many undercurrents here, she had strengthened them. She hoped so. There was need of all the strength she could muster to comfort Adelaide at this moment.

She wondered where Uncle Barney, Ben, Chris, and Ross were. Jethro had spoken of Todd but not of the others.

Tilda and Lizzie were standing on the porch as Meg got to the steps.

"Oh, Miss Meg, you are heaven-sent! Poor Miss Adelaide is just fit to be tied. She's carryin' on something terrible about that horse of hers. Millie's in there tryin' to get her to bed. It was bad enough yesterday, her and Todd comin' home from the funeral and findin' Mr. Barney and the boys taken in by the sheriff and his deputies!"

Meg gasped. "The sheriff!"

"Yes sirree. That new sheriff, Dan Cochran, and five deputies came out here and arrested 'em as nice as you please. Said it was something about them making their own money. There was a man with the sheriff who had come here all the way from Washington on account of some Donahue fake money. Imagine that! All that way to Indiana on account of the Donahues!"

Meg followed Tilda toward the door. Retribution tracked down every sinner in time, she thought. Grandma might have said, "As ye sow, so shall ye reap." What a miserable harvest Uncle Barney was reaping!

Dawn found Meg gazing out her window at the smoldering remains of the Donahue stables. By this time much of the crowd had dispersed. There had been nothing anyone could do. After she and Millie had gotten Adelaide quieted and to bed, Millie had told her that it was her opinion that the Indians had set the fire.

"And who could blame them, the way Mr. Barney treated them, cheating them forty ways from Sunday," the woman had said.

Meg sighed and turned from the window. More of that reaping-what-you-sow business, she supposed.

In the kitchen she found Mr. Lenfesty, Calvin, and Todd around the table, Tilda serving them breakfast. Meg exclaimed over Todd's bandaged hand and arm.

"I would have gladly burned both of them if I could have saved Harriet. How is Addie?" Todd asked her.

"Cried herself to sleep at last. I hope she sleeps all day." Meg got a cup, poured herself some coffee, and took the chair Calvin placed at the table for her.

Mr. Lenfesty looked at Todd. "What can we do for you, Todd, before we go home to our chores?"

"Nothing, I guess, Mr. Lenfesty. You folks were mighty neighborly to try to help us. I doubt if Pa would have done the same."

"What will you do now?" Calvin asked. "Now that—that——"

"Now that Pa and the boys are in jail?" Todd got up and walked to the fireplace, looked down at the blazing log a moment, then faced the table. "Well, I thought I'd get our men started at cleaning up. Then I'll go in town and see what's what with Pa. I expect it's the end of the line as far as he and the boys are concerned. I heard that Dan Cochran has collected considerable evidence in other matters than just the counterfeiting. I'm afraid there was quite a lot to collect in several categories."

"Will you rebuild the stables?" Calvin asked.

"Yes. I've got a plan of my own, if Pa and the boys don't come back. I want to raise horses on a big scale—do away with racing and just concentrate on breeding fine animals. Think I could do it, Cal?" Todd held his bandaged arm in his other hand as though it pained him.

Meg turned to Calvin and watched him rise and walk toward her cousin.

"Why not? You know horses as well as anyone in the county and you've got plenty of grazing land. Good idea, don't you think, Pa?"

Mr. Lenfesty stood. "Sycamore Park is a fine place to raise horses. Anything we can do to help you get started, Todd, why just call on us." He held out his hand.

Todd reached out his free hand and clasped Mr. Lenfesty's.

Meg's eyes met Tilda's. They both smiled. Meg knew she and Tilda had the same thought—how pleased Marietta must be to see her father shaking Todd's hand.

Meg followed Calvin and his father through the hall to the front door. Mr. Lenfesty said good-by and went out, leaving the door open.

Calvin hesitated, then closed the door and turned to Meg.

"Would it be all right if I came here to see you sometimes?" he asked.

"Of course. Bring Joyce too. I think it would be nice if she found out what kind of a man Todd is, don't you?"

He nodded. "Might be, at that. And Todd *is* a great fellow, just as you've told me all along." He smiled down at her. "Some of you Donahues are mighty fine folks." He put his hand on the doorknob.

"Calvin, Mrs. Eakins was telling me that you have been cutting a lot of timber on your land all winter. Going to build something?"

He put his cap on, then took it off quickly. "Well, yes, I am. I'm thinking about building a cabin, a small cabin on that rise beyond the wooded stretch."

"Maybe you'll show me the place, someday," Meg said boldly.

"Would you be interested, Meggy? It's going to be a very, *very*, small cabin," he emphasized, with a suggestion of a twinkle in his eyes.

"I'd be interested, Cal," Meg returned, her own eyes flashing brightly into his.

Calvin pulled on his cap, gave her a quick smile, then hurriedly dashed out the door.

Meg stood at the hall window and watched him run to catch up with his father, her heart a complex of sorrow and joy as the men passed the charred remains of the stables and then went on into the lane leading from Sycamore Park.